THE CODE OF HOPE

THE CODE OF HOPE

JORDYN FLEMING

©2025 Jordyn Fleming

Cover Illustration: Carrie-Rae Latham

Editing: Erika Steeves

Cover Design & Formatting: Susi Clark of Creative Blueprint Design

ISBN Paperback   979-8-9921245-0-7
ISBN Hardcover   979-8-9921245-1-4

CONTENTS

THE SANCTUARY OF TOMORROW

IRINA

S he should be here by now," I say, glancing down the alleyway. "Mom is never late."

Heath's eyes flit to me.

Any moment now, I expect to see her slipping through the shadows, moving with stealth and grace toward us. But she's nowhere to be seen.

As the sun begins to dip below the horizon, I realize that today will alter everything I've come to understand. Things can change so fast.

"Damn, we'll miss the boat," Heath says through clenched teeth, the words escaping more like a hiss. "If I could get my hands on Paul Randall, I'd throttle him."

"You and me both."

I remember exactly when I realized everything was about to change.

The memory of that day is etched vividly in my mind. It was an ordinary evening, and we were nestled on the cozy, rich brown leather sofa for movie night. Mom, Heath, and I were indulging in a bowl of buttery, golden popcorn when it happened. The screen went blue, followed by an ear-splitting screech. As the screen flickered, a message appeared, illuminating the features of Paul Randall, a polarizing politician. His thick chestnut hair was slicked back. He had a kind face and eyes that burned with an intense ambition that hinted at a desire for control.

That was the first announcement about mandated implants to reduce crime. I never expected him to be so persuasive or successful. It made me consider how there are moments when a situation appears so far-fetched that it forces you to confront the unsettling possibility of its realization. It's as if your body perceives an imminent upheaval, even if your conscious mind remains oblivious to what lies ahead. It was a stark realization of the regular people's lack of influence or how many agreed with these practices. The situation I had previously only seen in fiction—the swift erosion of my autonomy and rights—has now become a stark reality, unfolding at an alarming pace with the mere snap of someone's fingers.

"Give it a few more minutes. She'll be here," I say to the back of Heath's head. "And we'll be out of Paul Randall's clutches for good."

"Irina, we can't afford to wait any longer," Heath whispers, pressing me against the wall as a procession of the Sons of Paul strides past. The pristine white uniforms of the personnel are embellished with a remarkable depiction of a dove in red, white, and blue perched on a branch extending from a prominent vine over their right breast. It's been two weeks since Arkin broke away from the southeastern United States, transforming into its own distinct region. The Sons of Paul swiftly replaced traditional law enforcement agencies and emergency services, assuming all functions previously carried out by these institutions. The rest of the world is at a loss regarding how to aid or manage this newly formed entity.

The Sons of Paul members are not Implanted. These are the same individuals I went to school with. Even though I never belonged to the upper class, my mother ensured that Heath and I received a top-notch education. They now willingly support Paul Randall by carrying out roundups and subjecting others to a fate they managed to escape due to status. The idea makes me sick to my stomach.

"One more minute, please," I whisper, my fingers pressing into Heath's forearm. The taut, wiry muscles twitch under my touch.

His nostrils flare. "Fine."

I stand at the alleyway entrance, my eyes fixed on the dark shadows, waiting for her to appear. I try to stay composed, but the thought of leaving my mother behind tightens my chest, creating anxiety that also radiates from Heath. We stand together in tense silence, the two of us consumed by the same vigilance and desperate hope, knowing all too well the absurdity of our predicament.

Heath peers around the corner and glances back at me with deep-set green eyes. He runs his hands through his dark silky hair.

"One more minute," I plead.

His expression drops. "It's been two minutes, Irina."

I stand speechless, my mouth hanging open in disbelief. Our mother has always been our rock, but she insisted we leave without her if she didn't make it on time. The thought of leaving her behind in Arkin is too much.

"Should we go check the apartment first?" Heath rests his hand on my shoulders. "I understand it's a gamble."

I gaze into his determined eyes; an inner turmoil consumes me. Leaving now may please our mom, but abandoning her would fill me with regret and leave Heath guilt-stricken.

"We should check the apartment."

Our apartment's location is both a blessing and a curse. While it's conveniently located, it has been the target of multiple raids. Despite the constant threat of being caught, we've been fortunate to receive assistance, warnings, and support from like-minded individuals who refuse to be silenced.

He steals a glance at his watch. "We'll need to move fast. Otherwise, we won't reach the boat on time."

"Stick to the shadows."

Heath forces a smile, but his eyes remain cold as he clutches my elbow. His grip feels so tight that it cuts off the circulation in my arm. With a burst of energy, Heath pulls me along in a swift and agile stride. We press ourselves into the darkness of the alley, scurrying like frightened roaches, desperately avoiding any exposure that could lead to our demise.

Despite the mandate, Arkin's appearance remains virtually unchanged. The striking brown and red hues of the buildings' brick facades still dominate the urban landscape, while the sidewalks bear the marks of various substances, from discarded gum to lingering oil spills. At first glance, Arkin could easily be mistaken for any other city.

As we move along the shadows, our backs brushing against the towering buildings, we silently pass by a charming little coffee shop, Espresso-self, that once was my favorite Saturday morning spot. The deserted coffee mugs and discarded disposable cups scattered across the tables and floor create an unsettling atmosphere, as though the individuals who'd abandoned them departed in a hurry. I feel a piercing pang in my stomach as a myriad of memories come rushing back all at once.

"Irina, stop hanging back," Heath hisses through clenched teeth.

I glance down at my arm. He'd freed his grip.

"Sorry."

He follows my gaze to the abandoned espresso machine, and his eyes soften. Espresso-self still maintains its charm. The caramel-colored walls, chestnut espresso bar, and circular tables are all as they once were despite the disarray. The chalkboard with the week's specials still has writing across it. "Once we leave here, we'll have steaming cups of coffee waiting for us. We'll make new memories."

"I know. I just . . . liked it here."

"You're welcome to stick around," he quips with a poorly executed attempt at humor.

"Why? So, I can look like *them*?"

A steady stream of people are shuffling along the sidewalk up ahead, their movements strangely precise, almost robotic. Their vacant, distant expressions betray the telltale signs of the implant, rendering them unsettlingly detached from the world and the people around them.

Heath lets out a sigh. "Do you think you can mirror their facial expressions?"

"The frozen ones? Yeah."

"What about the movement and behavior?"

"Pretend I'm trapped in my head," I say, imitating their walk.

"Let me see the face."

I widen my eyes and allow the rest of my face to relax and go expressionless.

Heath flashes a confident grin. "Perfect. Alright, let's not waste any more time. If we don't match them, we're done for."

"You're really giving me this talk . . . again."

He nudges me with his elbow. "Just reminding you."

As we step out onto the sidewalk, I hold my breath, aware of the patterns of movement and expressions exhibited by the Implanted individuals around me. Their actions are mechanical, in stark contrast to the organic nature of human behavior. My heart flutters and I urge myself to stay composed, knowing that relying on prayer won't be enough to guide us through this.

We walk down the block, Heath in front acting as a shield against the various Sons of Paul groups we encounter.

There's a flutter in my chest as if a gust of wind has whisked away my breath. To regain my composure, I concentrate on planting my feet on the ground, fixing my gaze straight ahead, and concealing any trace of the turbulent emotions within me.

A piercing screech echoes across the entire area. Everyone comes to a coordinated halt as an announcement booms from overhead. Heath and I freeze, but perhaps a moment too late, which could spell trouble for us. The sound hangs in the air for an eternity, and I resist the urge to cover my ears. Then a man's voice reverberates over the speakers, casting a heavy shroud over everything. I recognize the voice, and a shiver runs through my body as every hair stands on end.

"Attention. The city's waterways are under strict guard, and all forms of transportation have been suspended," Paul Randall says. "Anyone attempting to leave the city will be apprehended and face the most severe repercussions."

Damn it. Our boat.

The severity of the most extreme punishment is unclear, but it will likely be more intricate than simply receiving an implant. Those who have managed to avoid this punishment so far are said to endure unspeakable acts that are not widely known to the public. Rumors have spread as some individuals defy Arkin's law.

As I stand here, I notice a sigh and a slight stumble nearby. Despite the instinct to look, I maintain a neutral expression and focus on the Sons of Paul converging on a bearded man. His slouched posture and sweat-drenched face indicate that he is un-Implanted.

The man attempts to flee, but it's apparent to any onlooker that he won't get far with the Sons of Paul so close. I watch with wide, unblinking eyes as the man is knocked to the ground, accompanied by a series of unsettling wet sounds.

Every fiber screams to turn away from the ghastly spectacle before me. But I have no choice but to watch as the man is yanked from the ground. A tear slips down my face. That's when the Implanted start moving again. Heath and I follow their lead, matching their stride. Neither of us says anything as we close the remaining distance to the apartment, not after what we witnessed the Sons of Paul do to the man.

The red brick of our building is now faded and discolored, casting a long rectangular shadow across the entire width of the street. Despite the chaos in adjacent streets, there are no signs of the Sons of Paul outside the building, and all seems quiet and undisturbed.

This is my home. I love it here. I love our neighbors and the memories and friends I made over the years. It's bittersweet to leave. When I finally moved out, I thought it would be because I'd found a place of my own and a decent job. Yet, that isn't the situation. Kids won't be leaving for college, their parents lingering in the driveway watching them drive away. All bittersweet moments of the past. Instead, those students and parents are either Implanted, captured, or sewer rats.

Sewer rats—that's our next step if we can't find a way out of here with the waterways closed and patrolled, I think.

I'm enveloped by the intense combination of mildew as I step into the lobby. The harsh glare of the fluorescent lights overhead feels almost blinding, casting the entire space in an otherworldly glow. To my left, the wall is painted with the imposing dove-and-vine emblem.

Heath swiftly scans the area as he seizes my hand and ushers me toward the narrow stairwell. His neck cranes as he vigilantly surveys every direction, especially over his shoulder. As soon as we're concealed from view, he cups my face in his hands, his touch assertive yet tender, compelling me to meet his gaze directly.

"Are you alright?"

"I think so," I whisper. In truth, I can't be sure if I am okay. Numbness has taken over, a reaction to the overwhelming fear. It feels like a form of disassociation, where I'm focused on survival and feel nothing else. My sole desire is to find Mom and make it to the boat alive.

"You might not be feeling alright at the moment, but I promise you'll be just fine once we get out of Arkin."

"We can't get out of here. The waterways are blocked," I remind him.

"There are other ways."

"If you say so."

I peer into his eyes, noticing a hint of lingering sadness. Over the last few weeks, I've observed Heath's adeptness at masking his feelings, always with a calm facade and a touch of humor, yet his eyes never fail to convey his genuine emotions. They now speak of a mixture of fear and profound disturbance.

His hands slip away from my face, leaving a lingering warmth. "It's time to go find Mom."

I try to mirror his smile, hoping to convey comfort, but I'm acutely aware of my failure.

"Find Mom. No wasting time," I say.

Heath nods.

We climb the stairs, our breath coming in ragged gasps as we take two steps at a time, desperate to close the distance to the fourth floor. We open the off-white door and enter the quiet hallway. The yellow light casts long shadows, and the only sound is the faint rustling from one of the rooms down the corridor. The worn blue carpet is marred by a jumble of stains, some old and faded and others disturbingly fresh.

Blood. A chill runs down my spine, and foreboding washes over me. My body tenses in anticipation of an unknown threat.

Just then, a Sons of Paul member steps out of a room at the far end of the hallway and into another. I stifle my scream and feel a rush of vomit claw at my mouth for escape. I don't know how I manage to stay hidden with my heart pounding so loudly.

Mom was probably captured, which would explain why she never showed. She must have sensed this possibility when she told us to leave without her, but we never took it that seriously. Mom is our superhero. But with the Sons of Paul roaming our building, she probably got stranded and had to hide.

I grasp the back of Heath's jacket and gently guide him into the first apartment on the right. It's a convenient entry point for us to strategize and develop a plan. The door is slightly ajar, revealing a room that has already been thoroughly ransacked. The shelves have been emptied of books, likely in a frantic search for money or anything of value that could be used as a bribe by those not implanted and seeking to escape Arkin. We cautiously make our way to the back room to avoid being overheard by the Sons of Paul. We navigate a sickening mix of soda and food matted into the carpet, barely avoiding the jagged edges of broken plates protruding from the mess.

"What's the plan?" I ask.

Heath absentmindedly strokes his patchy facial hair, deep in thought. "I'm not sure," he murmurs.

"Our apartment is two doors down."

"You're stating the obvious. I can count," he snaps.

"Look, I'm just as stressed as you, but desperate times call for a plan, sometimes a desperate, reckless plan."

"Do you have a plan?"

"I do. You won't like it."

Heath cocks his head to the side. "Spill. Our options are limited."

"I suggest we use the split-up method. One of us creates a diversion while the other checks the apartment for signs of intrusion. It's not the most detailed plan, but it's the best I've got for now."

"You're right. I despise that idea, yet it seems to be our only option."

"We may not all make it out."

"Irina, I won't entertain that kind of thinking," Heath asserts, his tone more akin to that of a protective older brother rather than a younger sibling.

"Fine. Think positive," I say to myself. "What role would you rather play?"

"I'd rather be the ruse. You look for Mom."

"What's the sign I should be looking for?"

"When the fire alarm sounds, that's your cue."

I tilt my head and conjure a strained smile before replying, "Understood."

"I'll be back," Heath says, going to the main door. "Let's meet at the hiding place." He peers through the crack and, when the coast is clear, slips out.

The hiding place is concealed within a tight corner that remains a secret shared exclusively with those who understand its significance. A musty odor lingers there, a testament to the passage of time and neglect, yet it's consistently provided refuge and protection. Accessible only through a low crouch and a crawl, this discreet and secure passage offers a covert escape. Its original purpose remains mysterious, as the building's long history spans over a century.

I find a secluded corner and press myself against the wall, drawing comfort from its curved surface, which surrounds me like a protective embrace. As I wait for the signal, I close my eyes and start counting backward from one hundred, each number echoing in my mind as I wait. With each passing moment, my nerves intensify, and I'm keenly aware of the time slipping away.

The shrill sound of the fire alarm pierces through the apartment, sending a jolt of urgency through the still air. The warning lights overhead cast an eerie glow as they flash frantically, signaling imminent danger. I pause for a breath, my heart racing, as the unmistakable sound of footsteps echoes down the hallway, drawing closer. With cautious determination, I poke my head out the door, scanning the corridor for movement.

Steeling myself, I slip into apartment 403. The familiar surroundings are a haunting reminder of the chaos brought about by the Sons of Paul and the great upheaval. Each step takes me deeper into the heart of my home, and a surge of bitter frustration washes over me as I survey the disarray that has marred the once pristine space. Cherished memories now feel tainted by the disorder and disruption left in the wake of the Sons of Paul.

As the seconds tick by, my anxiety spikes as I frantically search through every room, hoping to catch a glimpse of Mom. My heart feels heavier with each passing moment, and a dread engulfs me. My hands tremble as I mentally prepare to leave the apartment and go to the hiding place to wait for Heath, until a realization strikes me.

Mom is petite, barely reaching five feet. When I was young, whenever we played hide-and-seek, she always had a unique hiding spot she loved to use.

I rush to the closet and fling open the door. Inside, I pull aside the topmost layer of a large bin of clothes.

"Mom?"

My mother's head pops up, and her dark brown eyes widen in surprise. "Irina, you shouldn't be here."

"We came back for you."

Her disapproving cluck of the tongue echoes in the room. "You're going to get caught. You should have heeded my advice and left when you had the chance."

I gaze steadily at her, searching for an answer. "Would you have left us?"

"That's different. You two are my children."

"And you're our mom."

"Alright," Mom says, reaching for my hand. "Help me get out of here."

"Are you okay?" I grip Mom's arm as I help her step out, holding her steady until she gets her bearings.

"Folding this body up at this age has its downfalls," she says, smiling.

"We have to meet Heath at the hiding place," I say.

Her eyes narrow. "He set the fire alarm."

"He could already be there."

"Let's not waste any more time."

I cling to Mom, my heart racing as we walk through the hallway. As we press on, the shrill wail of the fire alarm fills the air, drowning out all other sounds. The bright emergency lights flash, casting a glow that illuminates the surroundings. With each step, the urgency mounts, driving us forward until we reach the safety of our hiding place. As we arrive, the distant sound of approaching footsteps sends a chill down my spine.

I pull with all my strength on the stubborn little door. Tension builds in my chest as I struggle to open it. When it finally gives way, a wave of relief washes over me. Mom's small but strong hands push me into the cramped hiding spot, but from there, I can see Heath sprinting down the hallway toward us.

"Go!" Heath yells.

As the Sons of Paul draw nearer, my mother's body tenses and her back straightens. She fixes me with a last, lingering look, her eyes filled with a profound burden.

"We won't all make it out alive, my dear," she whispers with tears in her eyes. "I love you."

"Mom, we can't think like that," I say, remembering Heath's words. "We'll stick together, no matter what."

"Not today." She gives me a sad smile before shutting the door.

The moisture in my mouth has turned viscous, and a sensation of constriction grips my throat. Breathing in feels like a struggle, as if my lungs are filling with sand. I keep looking at the tiny square-shaped door. I can't open it from my current position. It's impossible.

Then a cacophony of shouts followed by heavy thuds and the jostling of bodies intertwine with the sounds of a fierce struggle playing out over the fire alarm in the distance. My heart races faster. After a deep breath, I finally swallow and regain my composure.

"I love you," I whisper. "I'll make this right."

As much as I detest the idea, crawling seems to be my only means of escape. Despite the impossible odds, I plan to seek out an elusive group known as The Shield. While Paul Randall may view them as rebels, I see them as the key to preserving humanity and civilization.

I'll do everything in my power to free Mom and Heath, and to instill the sanctuary of tomorrow.

SHADOWS FADING

EVANDER

Hearing Evander's calm voice, the group braced themselves as he whispered, "One, two, three, go!"

They emerged one by one from the dim, clammy sewer, striding down a poorly illuminated alley. Their footfalls scarcely disturbed the rugged pavement as they hastened from one shadowy recess to the next, searching for cover. The ground was cloaked in a grimy film of thick, dark oil that seeped into every crevice. The air hung thick with the sickening reek of decomposing garbage, making it almost unbearable to draw in a breath.

"You look green," Madison said.

Evander's stomach churned as he fought to suppress the acrid taste burning his throat. When he'd first sought refuge in the dark, dank sewers, he believed the putrid stench would toughen him and he'd become impervious to the noxious fumes. To his dismay, the opposite was true. He found himself growing more sensitive and intolerant to the relentless assault on his senses. It was as though each odor had intensified, overwhelming him with its potency. He began to suspect that it wasn't just the foul air in the sewers but perhaps a primal instinct for self-preservation causing his heightened sensitivity.

"Just a different set of smells, and not good ones," he said.

As they grappled with the unforgiving truth of their circumstances, Evander and his companions—Madison, Brooks, and Jett—had come to the stark realization that securing more food was necessary for survival. With the specter of starvation looming over them, they'd ventured up into the desolate streets in a desperate quest for sustenance. The harrowing experience of living in the sewers had exacted a heavy physical and mental toll on their bodies, rendering them feeble and gaunt, particularly distressing considering the two vulnerable children within their group. Evander was barely twenty, making him the oldest, and Madison, barely a teenager, had a natural way with the boys, who were eight and seemed to be developing a sense of maturity beyond their years. The world's harsh realities had already begun to erase the youthful innocence from their faces, leaving behind a more hardened and weathered facade.

Despite the foul stench wafting from the overflowing garbage bins, they continued sifting through what seemed like mountains of waste. Ordinarily, they would have avoided the really rank bins, but their desperate urgency propelled them to rummage through even the most unsanitary ones.

"It's almost like they're hiding discarded food just so we end up either starving or selling ourselves to them," Madison said, her hands splattered with brown goo.

"It might be part of their master plan," Evander said.

"They could only hope," Madison replied. "Do you think the Implanted eat?"

"They'd have to. They're still human."

Evander raised the lid and recoiled as a wave of the most pungent odor yet assailed his senses. Undeterred, he persevered with his search until he eventually spotted a piece of bread tucked away in the corner. The bread was adorned with intricate patterns of green and white mold, its edges charred and blackened as if a desperate attempt had been made to salvage its edibility by toasting it. Meanwhile, Madison unearthed a forgotten bag of potato chips, stale and lackluster. Though their discoveries were meager, they offered at least a modicum of sustenance that would momentarily alleviate the gnawing hunger in their stomachs.

"Things aren't so bad," Evander said reassuringly as he raised the bread above his head.

The sight of food caused Brooks' and Jett's eyes to light up.

"Just when I thought we'd be going to bed with stomach thunder again," Madison said.

Evander chuckled. They'd coined the phrase "stomach thunder" about a month ago when food supplies started running low. Throughout the night, their stomachs rumbled and grumbled, vying for attention as they all tried to find sleep.

"There's an abandoned store over there; let's head in for a moment so we can eat." Evander took the lead, as he often did.

They were met with cobwebs draped across the corners and shelves teeming with a diverse array of dusty, abandoned items. With each tentative step, they journeyed toward the recesses of the musty store, reaching the far-right corner at the back, where they stumbled upon a small, hidden alcove. Here, nestled out of sight, they sought solace amid the clutter of vacant crates and weathered boxes that occupied the space.

Madison tore the loaf of bread into four equal portions. She verified that each piece was as nearly identical as possible and counted out the golden chips, ensuring everyone would receive a fair share. While they ate, they engaged in subdued conversations, aware of the necessity to evade unwelcome attention.

"This is tasty," Brooks exclaimed with his mouth full of bread. He always devoured food as soon as it landed in his hands.

"I wish we had bread every day," Jett said.

As hard as they tried to avoid detection and evade being implanted, Evander couldn't shake the feeling that their chances of survival were slipping away by the hour. With scarce nourishment, every moment felt like an exhausting battle, and hopelessness loomed over them. Despite this, Evander made the difficult decision to bear this burden alone, not wanting to dampen their spirits, especially Brooks and Jett. Without a reliable source of food, their hopes of escaping the clutches of the Sons of Paul and breaking free from the implants would be futile.

He cast a fleeting glance in Madison's direction, taking in her slender frame and delicate appearance. It conveyed a fragility that made her appear as if she might shatter at the slightest misstep.

"Is everyone done?" Evander asked. "We need to move soon." The two boys were seated next to each other, whispering. They leaned against the wall with their legs stretched out as they enjoyed the fresh air. "The next sewer entrance is located to the right. We'll need to move fast."

Madison looked at the two younger boys. "We're done."

With utmost caution, they formed a single-file line to navigate the narrow, labyrinthine alleyways. A palpable urgency filled the air. They couldn't enter back the way they had come, just in case—they never knew who was watching. Each winding path offered a temporary refuge from the unwavering gaze of the Sons of Paul, yet every step bore the weight of potential discovery. Assuming the role of the vanguard, Evander charted their course through the twisting passages. The resolve in his eyes was matched only by the wariness of his calculated movements.

Their progress was halted by the resounding clatter and skittering of a metal can on the unforgiving concrete. Evander knew that any such disturbance could attract the attention of the relentless agents of the Sons of Paul, who patrolled the streets looking for any hint of dissent. Amid the programmed grace of the Implanted's movements, an insignificant and chaotic sound, such as metal clattering, could only be attributed to the clandestine maneuvers of the rebels, serving as a reminder of the dangerous dance they conducted in the shadows.

Evander's fingers closed around Madison's arm, and she stumbled backward. She scanned the area for Jett, who reached out and grabbed Brooks. They all froze and held their breath as approaching footsteps grew louder.

"The can is there," a voice said.

"They're nearby."

Sons of Paul.

Evander squeezed his eyes shut, trying to block out the terrifying reality closing in on them. The Sons of Paul, and their unwavering determination to gain Paul Randall's favor, posed a significant threat to the un-Implanted, as they employed increasingly violent and unscrupulous tactics.

His mind raced as he struggled to come up with a plan to escape the clutches of their oppressors. The thought of their capture sent a deep chill down his spine, knowing the grave dangers that awaited them. His heart ached for Jett and Brooks, who still clung to their innocence, their vulnerable spirits at risk of being callously exploited. The cruel fate that awaited them, the prospect of being forcibly implanted without a second thought for their well-being, weighed heavily on Evander. As for himself and Madison, the consequences of capture were even more staggering. He knew that if caught, they would likely face unspeakable punishment at the hands of the tyrannical Sons of Paul and be made an example of to strike fear into the hearts of other rebels. They had to act swiftly, but he had no clue how.

An unfamiliar voice called out, causing Evander to jerk his head up. Before him stood a menacing soldier, grinning with a terrifyingly sinister look. "They're here!"

The realization dawned on Evander like a mist rolling in from the horizon: he hadn't acted fast enough, and they were trapped. The group stood frozen in place. Evander took a deep breath and positioned himself in front of the others. He scanned the area, searching for more Sons of Paul, but only one figure had seen them. "Run!" Evander ordered.

His directive ignited a fire in the other three, and they scattered; he only hoped they'd make it away from this man and back to the sewers.

"Oh no you don't," a different voice said.

Jett squirmed and struggled to break free from the grip of another soldier, who held the boy up as if he had just captured the ultimate prize and was determined to hold onto it at all costs. The man's pristine white uniform enveloped Jett, almost seeming to swallow him up. Evander's attention was momentarily diverted as he caught a glimpse of a bird—was that a dove?—perched on a delicate vine, and the sight struck him as a strange emblem.

Standing helplessly, Evander watched Jett's futile attempts to escape, and it brought home the unfairness of it all. At that moment, Evander felt powerless, realizing he had nothing to offer the Sons of Paul in exchange for Jett's freedom. All he could do was watch, his heart aching for the young boy's predicament.

"Please let him go," Evander pleaded to the Sons of Paul as another immobilized him from behind.

Just when Evander had nearly given up hope, a glass bottle plummeted from above them and shattered off to the side. The loud crash echoed through the narrow alley, and a billowing cloud of vibrant pink smoke began to spread, obscuring everything in its path until it engulfed the entire alleyway. Amid the chaos, the pungent aroma of burning chemicals hung heavily in the air, making every breath a struggle. The otherworldly glow of the pink smoke transformed the surroundings into a surreal and unsettling spectacle. As Evander struggled to escape the soldier's grip, a cacophony

THE CODE OF HOPE

of voices, grunts, and muffled sounds of impact echoed in the background, creating a chaotic symphony that intensified the tension in the air. Evander threw his head back and heard a sickening crunch. The grip around him loosened, and Evander was able to break free. Blood spilled down the soldier's face.

"When I get my hands on you—"

Without thinking, Evander lunged at him, driving the soldier to the ground, and delivered a decisive blow to the man's face, knocking him unconscious. He gathered his resolve and slowly rose to his feet, the ground beneath him feeling unsteady.

Determined to locate Jett and the rest of the group and escape from the haze, Evander extended his arm and cautiously moved forward, his eyes stinging from the smoke. Despite the challenging visibility, a glimmer of hope ignited within him, as if a silent benefactor had sensed his desperation and was leading him toward a potential escape route.

"What are you doing?" a woman's voice hissed. "Go the other way! They won't be out for long!"

Evander searched for the origin of the lingering voice. A young woman materialized from the pink smoke. Her lustrous dark brown hair was silky and neatly fastened in a braid, with a few wisps framing her face. She wore an ensemble of loose-fitting jeans and a snug sweatshirt. She was holding onto Jett's arm as she emerged from the haze and guided him behind her.

"Where am I supposed to go?" Evander said.

Her other hand shot out without hesitation, fingers curling around the fabric of Evander's shirt sleeve with a firm grip. She pulled him forward, propelling them through the billowing smoke. The woman moved ahead without glancing back. Evander followed, stealing a quick glance at Jett, whose wide eyes betrayed an unmistakable fear as he kept his gaze straight ahead.

The sound of raised voices increased with each passing moment. Despite the escalating commotion, the woman leading the way remained remarkably composed. She navigated the convoluted passages with purposeful strides, guiding them to an unassuming building that appeared to be an abandoned restaurant, but upon closer inspection it revealed itself to be a silent and dormant coffee shop. Espresso-self, the tattered sign read. The stillness of the espresso machines hinted at a latent energy, as if they were waiting to be awoken once more. Maintaining a steady grip on her companions, the woman brought them past the shop's entrance and down a flight of stairs.

The musty aroma of well-aged coffee beans filled Evander's senses, sending a wave of surprise through him. The scent was so potent he could almost taste the earthy bitterness of the coffee on the tip of his tongue. The anticipation of enjoying a freshly brewed cup made his mouth water.

"Evander!" Madison said, jumping to her feet and throwing her arms around him.

He hugged Madison back. "I guess we should thank you," he said, gesturing toward the woman.

"Irina," she said, enunciating the name, then shifted her focus to Madison. "I'm happy that you, at least, can follow directions."

Madison shrugged.

"Irina," Evander repeated. "Why did you save us? You could have been caught, too."

Irina shrugged. "I like to help people."

"You risked yourself."

Irina stood up straight. "When my mom and brother were captured, I felt so helpless, like I couldn't do anything to save them. So be grateful that you're safe now."

"I appreciate your help. It's just that most people don't bother to help anymore," Evander said.

Irina grabbed a few items from the shelves and said, "Most people can't help you. They're under the control of Paul Randall." She paused for a moment. "The ones who can help are hiding and surviving, or they're part of The Shield."

"The Shield?" Evander and Madison asked in unison. Brooks and Jett clung to their legs.

"It's the resistance. They operate underground."

Evander stepped toward her. "The rebels?"

"If you want to call them that, then sure," Irina said.

"So you're part of The Shield?" Madison asked.

"Is that a surprise?" Irina raised her pierced eyebrow.

Madison started to wring her pale hands together, as she often did when nervous. "You're just so young," she said.

Irina furrowed her brows, her expression grave. "It doesn't matter how old or young you are. If you've evaded them this long, the Sons of Paul won't stop until they capture you. That propaganda trying to convince people like you that children are safe once captured isn't true; they don't care about that. Anyone can be tortured and implanted—then they're trapped as any regular Implanted but must live with the pain of the torture they experienced, too."

Evander stood frozen in shock, unable to comprehend the words he was hearing. "Kids? They'd do such a thing to *kids*?" His mind reeled at the thought of children being subjected to such heinous treatment—it was inconceivable. He shoved his hands into his pants pockets, trying to ground himself. He shifted his weight back and forth on his feet, feeling the weight of disbelief and outrage settling heavily upon him.

"They do it to kids all the time."

Evander ran his hands through his greasy hair. "Do we stay here for the night?"

Irina laughed.

Evander smiled. "Is that a yes?"

"That's a hell no." Irina's eyes flitted over the group. She shrugged off her backpack and rummaged through it. Eventually, she found what she was looking for, two rectangular packages. She extended one to Brooks and the other to Jett. "Granola bar?"

The boys nearly ripped her hands off as they swiped the food from her.

She looked at Evander and Madison. "I don't have anything else, but once we get to where we're going, you'll be fed. If we make it there."

"If?" Madison said.

"Yep. We should probably get going. They'll be through here anytime now," Irina said.

Irina made her way to a small cabinet so insignificant that one would need to crouch down to see it. She took out a gleaming object from her pocket and skillfully inserted it into what looked like a lock. Evander found it peculiar that such an inconspicuous cabinet would need a lock. He probably wouldn't have noticed it if Irina hadn't pointed it out; it was easy to miss. Then, a metal *click*, and Irina returned the key to her pocket.

She pulled open the wooden cabinet doors, turned, and smiled at the group. "Off you go," she said.

Madison tilted her head, a perplexed expression on her face. "We're supposed to hide in a cabinet?"

"You're supposed to go through it. Squat down," Irina directed.

Evander slowly lowered himself into a crouch. The hole was so narrow his shoulders would barely fit without rubbing the sides. "Where does it go?"

"In a little way. Then you'll come across a ladder that you'll go down," Irina said as if she had explained this a million times.

"What stops them from tipping the cabinet over and discovering the hole in the wall?" Madison asked.

"You don't know much about how things happened here, do you? Anyway, most business owners assemble their furniture on the walls. As far as the tunnels? That's beyond me, but you can ask questions to The Shield once we're there." The boys had finished their granola bars, and Irina collected the trash from them, shoving it in the sides of her backpack.

"I'll go with her," Jett announced, stepping forward.

"Me too," Brooks said.

Evander nodded. "I'll go first," he said, stepping up. "Do I just crawl through there?"

"That's right," Irina said. "Take this."

Evander took the headlamp from Irina's outstretched hand, then positioned it atop his head and came down on all fours. Jett and Brooks took the next strap and crawled through the narrow hole after him. He anticipated this would be a difficult task due to the size of the opening and his weight, but he was determined to persevere, considering everything he had already endured. The air carried a musty odor of mildew and dirt, but he pressed on through the confined space, glad he wasn't claustrophobic. He could hear Jett's quiet breaths and movements behind him.

"You okay, buddy?"

"Yeah. It stinks."

"Worse than the sewers?"

Jett released a small laugh. "No way!"

"The sewers smell like poop," Brooks shouted.

Evander noticed a black circle and gray bars curved above it up ahead. "We're at the ladder. I'll go down before you. Just stay focused and don't look down."

"Okay," Madison's voice came to him from behind Brooks. "I'm a little nervous."

"That's okay. Nerves mean you're not Implanted, right?" Evander said.

"Right."

As Evander descended the rusty ladder, the cold metal bit into his palms with each deliberate movement. He fought to keep his composure, not knowing how far down this went, and took slow, deep breaths to steady his nerves. The creaks and groans of the metal ladder echoed through the dark shaft, adding to the oppressive atmosphere. Finally, after what seemed like an eternity, his feet made contact with solid ground, and he released a long, shuddering sigh of relief. Next came Jett, then Brooks, followed by Madison, and finally Irina, their figures becoming more distinct as they descended into the darkness.

Once they were all on the ground, Irina gestured for them to proceed. Evander stepped into the abyss first, shivering as a rush of frigid air enveloped him. The environment belowground was naturally distinct, with the air noticeably colder, and apart from the faint light emanating from the headlamps they were surrounded by pitch black. Every step felt like a plunge into the unknown, the darkness seeming to swallow everything in its path.

Evander looked in Irina's direction, wanting to know more about her. "So, you said your mom and brother were captured?"

"They were."

"Early on?"

She shook her head as if lost in thought. "It depends," she said, her forehead wrinkling. "When we were trying to escape, most people had been Implanted. It was still early on, during the initial phase. We were scheduled to leave to start a new life. We had a way out, but it didn't work."

"What happened?"

Irina was focused on a point in the distance as she spoke. "Our apartment was raided. Word got out that we were a sanctuary of sorts, and we became a target. Most people had already left or been captured the day my mom was at the apartment. That's when another raid happened, right when she was scheduled to meet us. She hid because she had no time to flee."

Evander ran his hand through his unkempt hair. "Where were you and your brother?"

"A few blocks away. We were supposed to leave if Mom didn't arrive on time, but we couldn't do it." She laughed. "Mom would have been okay with us leaving her; she told us to. She would have taken solace in knowing or hoping that we'd escaped Arkin, but we wouldn't have been okay knowing we had left her there . . . here. Heath . . . we went back for her. To the apartment. I found her, but time or luck wasn't on our side. Heath was chased and Mom pushed me through the hidden exit and locked me in before the Sons of Paul could see . . . They were caught. I fled."

Madison's voice was filled with empathy as she asked, "Have you had a chance to see them again since?"

"I have. They weren't the same. I saw recognition in their eyes, making me believe they were still somewhere." She looked Evander in the eye. "I think that while Paul Randall has a certain level of control over the Implanted, it's incomplete. I'll free them from that prison."

Madison stepped to the other side of Irina since the pathway had widened up a bit. "You think there's a cure, a way to free the Implanted?"

"I don't know of a cure, but The Shield and I believe they can be freed. We just haven't figured out how."

Evander's heart raced as he processed the information—a possible escape from the unrelenting challenges of this world. Thoughts rushed through his mind in a whirlwind of hope and disbelief as he grappled with the enormity of the news. Amid the tumult of his emotions, he blurted out what he knew was the most critical question of his life. "Is there anything we can do to help?"

"Well, you don't get sanctuary with The Shield without help. You find others like us, and you toss out ideas. You start by finding people, like I did today, observing the Implanted, and bringing any information or detection to The Shield to be studied or considered," Irina said, slowing their pace and veering down a dark hallway branching off from the main path.

Evander shook his head. "What about the kids?"

Irina looked at the boys, then at Madison. "They get to be kids."

Evander smiled. "This sounds too good to be true."

They finally reached a door and Irina rapped a strange sequence. Despite their headlamps, seeing or making out any details was complicated. "You'll see soon enough," she said as the door opened, flooding them with heavenly light. "Welcome home."

EDEN FALLING

KINLEY

Sunlight. Clouds. Yellow. White. Smile.

Every day, my body operates like clockwork as I mechanically make my way to the factory I am assigned. I move without conscious control, almost as if I'm on autopilot—the factory changes every week, following a rotation schedule. It's programmed into the implant. Whatever is typed in their system registers to the respective group. The Implanted produce everything for Paul Randall.

Right. Left. One step. Two steps.

Every movement is steady, as if my body were automatic and without a mind. And who am I kidding? I never gave much thought to what autopilot meant while I was in foster care and heard my peers describe that as the mode in which they functioned. I never felt that way; I survived until I was alone for a few months. But here I am now, on autopilot.

But autopilot isn't what I thought it'd be. I operate subconsciously, automatically, under the control of the implant while fully aware of my surroundings. I didn't know awareness would be part of it. There's a disconnect between my mind and body. I'm a passenger on a ride I can't control.

Jeans. Faded.

Nod.

Hello, I say in my head. There's no point in trying to vocalize it; it wouldn't work.

I long to engage in spoken conversation. I never realized how I would yearn for simple verbal interaction.

From the moment I was Implanted, my autonomy disappeared. Now, I feel like a hollow shell of who I used to be. I can vividly recall being led into the cold, sterile room where the implantation procedure took place. The environment mirrored the starkness of my current existence. Unable to choose, I was among the initial group to undergo implantation. I was on the brink of aging out of the foster care system when I found myself under the control of Paul Randall. They handed me over. I was used as a guinea pig, a person without any support or care. I was an experiment. The foster care system abandoned me and left me in the hands of someone I didn't know.

After the implant was activated, I lost control over every movement of my body. It felt like I was enclosed in a capsule, isolated within the limits of my mind. The first-generation implants, including my own, put considerable strain on the body and resulted in a high mortality rate; the design and capabilities had to be reevaluated. At least, that's what I've overheard among the un-Implanted under Paul Randall's control; he calls them his branches. Whatever that means.

While my body mechanically navigates through the city, I consciously try to smile and greet others, even though it's purely a mental exercise. This routine anchors me, grounds me in reality amid the implant's authoritarian control over my physical actions.

I mentally narrate physical actions. It's like a fleeting glimpse of humanity. A desperate attempt to cling to normalcy amid the chaos of life. Does anyone else experience this?

It's an improvement from the mental screams and despair . . .

Red. Glasses.

Good morning.

In Arkin, even the most ordinary activities seem out of sync, particularly when there's a procession from the Sons of Paul parading through the streets. They loom like an ominous thunderhead, poised to disrupt anyone's intentions. As members of the Implanted, we craft their impeccable uniforms. Sometimes, I daydream about smearing spaghetti or ice cream on those pristine white garments, imagining the astonishment on their faces—wide-eyed, mouths agape, unable to comprehend what happened. The thought alone makes me wish I could laugh.

Right. Left.

As my body navigates the city streets, I notice that the route I'm taking today differs from the one I traveled last week. This time, I find myself heading toward the East. The factories in the city's East district are dedicated to luxury or high-end goods specifically requested by Paul Randall. This shift in my work assignment is a breath of fresh air compared to last week's monotonous tasks. Instead of assembling shiny metal parts while enduring the discomfort and pain in my hands and fingers, I'm now immersed in creating exquisite products with prestige and importance.

The towering skyscrapers on this side of the city are awe-inspiring. Their mirrored surfaces reflect the sunlight with a surreal brilliance. The air here is pure and refreshing, in contrast with the smoky, polluted atmosphere in the West district. This area is maintained, likely due to the absence of rebels who tend to avoid this section. No litter or remnants of smoke bombs. It's a risky area for rebels to venture into, and the chances of being seen or apprehended are significantly higher.

The enormous rectangular factory looms in the distance. Its sheer size is overwhelming and it dominates the landscape. I still have about a quarter of a mile to cover before I reach the entrance, and I can see a few other people walking along the sidewalk, slightly ahead of me and others behind. In total, only a handful of us are making our way to the factory.

There's a faint rustling between the two towering buildings to my right. In the past, I would have moved away, fearing the presence of someone with malicious intent. However, in my current state, I cannot take any action.

"Now, now, now!" a woman says.

Two figures with their faces obscured by sinister masks throw themselves at me, their movements efficient. They easily overpower me with surprising strength and precision.

I can't help but wonder if they are agents of the Sons of Paul who discarded their blindingly white uniforms. My mind races with questions.

What do they intend to do with me?

In this world, some still see the Implanted as easy prey. Those without implants can act with free will and target those who are Implanted. Members of the Sons of Paul might do it for amusement or out of cruelty, using their ruthless methods to avoid getting caught. If they are extensions or branches of Paul Randall, whatever sinister purpose lies in the back of his mind must be horrible.

The two figures slip a rough burlap sack over my head, plunging me into disorienting darkness.

"Please be gentle with her. We need to ensure she doesn't get hurt," a woman's voice urges.

"I never intended to harm her. What will we do with her?" *Rebels.*

"We should observe her, analyze her behavior, and determine what useful information we can gather. Perhaps we can appeal to release her. What do you think, Evander?" the woman asks.

Their voices blend, creating a comforting melody. I capture the nuances of their dialogue, from the rise and fall of their intonation to the subtle inflections that reveal layers of their personalities. Each exchange is seamless, with no awkward pauses, only a natural and captivating rhythm.

Their cold, clammy hands wrap around my upper arms, gripping me as they guide me forward. A jolt of electricity surges through me. My legs stiffen and become almost unresponsive, as if my body is shutting down. Every movement is an immense effort, like my muscles are turning into heavy concrete. I am consumed by total helplessness. At that moment, I yearn to take control of my body.

"Well, that's unfortunate," the woman says.

"Irina, what do we do?" Evander asks. He sounds panicked. Worried.

"Something I hoped we could avoid, but oh well."

The peripheries of my sight darken and become hazy, merging into a central focal point, and my body becomes increasingly heavy and unresponsive.

* * *

As my eyes open, I am surrounded by the enveloping darkness within the confines of the burlap sack. The air is cool against my skin, and I can sense the stark contrast in temperature from where I was taken to the unfamiliar location where I find myself. A soft cushion provides some comfort against my back, but I'm restrained and disoriented. My arms are strapped to the armrests of a chair.

"Irina, Evander, where did you find this one?" a woman asks, her voice different from the previous speaker.

So, that's her name. *Irina*.

"East," Irina says.

"Heading to the East is quite risky. If Rebecca comes to know about it, she might confiscate your exterior passes."

"Chey, we must keep this information between ourselves—the three of us," Evander says.

Chey.

The woman, Chey, lets out a deep, exasperated sigh. "What am I supposed to do with her?"

"Try to disable the implant," Irina says as if it were the simplest thing in the world.

"We don't have all the information we need about the implant. I'm concerned that moving forward with this could pose a significant risk."

"Is there another way to learn about them without attempting it?" Irina asks. "As long as we aren't moving her around and her face is covered, we're golden. Also, she can't necessarily move since she's bound."

"This isn't ethical, though," Chey argues, her voice shaking with emotion.

"Chey," Irina continues, "it's important to remember that this decision is for the greater good."

I find myself absorbed in their conversation to the point where I forget that the topic of discussion is my future. There's a weighty thought looming in my mind—am I comfortable with risk, knowing the potential consequences? What could be worse than feeling like a captive within my own body? I'm eager for them to unravel the mystery surrounding the implants. If I could participate in the initial experimental phase, I'd willingly embrace the opportunity to be part of this groundbreaking liberation experiment. I don't have a choice; I'm a voiceless participant.

Their voices are barely above a whisper as they continue to engage in a passionate yet tense discussion. The air is thick with the palpable tension between them, each of their words laced with emotion. They speak over each other in a desperate attempt to convey their perspective, but it only adds to the feeling of conflict in the room. It's as if their words are hissing at each other, and no one's listening to the other's point of view. The mounting tension makes me want to break free from this suffocating atmosphere and escape. Conflict has never been my preferred way of communicating.

"Alright, that's enough. Evander and I will accompany her back to the exterior," Irina says. "I'll set her free there. Once this is taken care of, you won't be responsible anymore. But remember, don't approach me when you regret your decision later."

The gravity of her words makes it clear there is no room for debate regarding her choice.

"Irina," Chey says, "I just want to clarify that I'm not opposed to your idea. I just feel like I can't proceed with the experiment without consent from the person involved. If something were to go wrong, I'd feel guilty. I don't want to be seen as someone who didn't give them a choice, right from the beginning."

"Obtaining consent? How can you expect consent when they have no control over the situation? It's Paul Randall who has all the control!" As she spoke, I heard something clatter across the room.

"Irina . . ." Chey says.

"I understand where she's coming from," Evander jumps in, a note of concern in his voice. "We can't keep waiting for consent that may never come. We need to find another way to approach this."

"You've adopted her tough demeanor even though you haven't been here for very long," Chey says.

Irina sighs. "Chey, I'm not trying to be tough or inconsiderate of these people, but we have to do *something*. Obtaining consent is . . . far-fetched."

"I understand," Chey says, her voice tinged with uncertainty. "I'd feel better about it if we had a sign."

"We'll take her back, and once you've got your sign, we'll attempt to capture another one. However, we won't have any information about the variant. At least in this case, we have some knowledge," Irina says.

As I concentrate, I can't help but wonder about the motivation that led Paul Randall to distance himself from these first-generation implants, even though they marked the downfall of others. There must be a hidden flaw or vulnerability that he knows about, a potential loophole in the system. If there were, he'd never share it.

At this moment, I sense an unparalleled opportunity to test and exceed my capabilities. I vividly recall my initial struggle to break free from the restraints, which proved futile and painful. But now I'm fueled by a profound purpose transcending my existence—the emancipation of individuals like me and every inhabitant of Arkin. I can do this. I have a purpose. I need to let them know I'm willing to embrace the role of the experiment, for the greater good.

I focus my mind on the delicate action of shifting just one finger. I maintain an optimistic mindset and direct my mental energy toward my hand, urging it to respond. I intensify my concentration, focusing entirely on my fingers and the intricate network of fibers that govern their movement. It's imperative that I communicate my willingness to support the resistance.

The intense wave of nausea churning in my stomach is overwhelming, as if a tumultuous storm is brewing deep within. Agonizing pain throbs in my skull, sending stabs throughout my entire head. It feels as though my mind and body are being torn apart. I find myself struggling against the small device that cruelly exerts complete control over me, yearning with every fiber of my being to break free from its unyielding grip.

And that's when it happens.

I feel it.

A slight twitch in my index finger. It's subtle, barely noticeable, but it assures me that I can replicate it again.

As I deeply engross myself in the demanding task, an intense pang shoots through me. Despite the overwhelming and relentless pain, I summon all my determination and continue to push, resolute in my decision to endure the discomfort. It dawns on me that this intense level of concentration might be what led to the demise of the other implants like mine. Perhaps they had stumbled upon a potential breakthrough but pushed their bodies beyond their limits. And yet, amid the physical discomfort, the implant retains its hold on me, despite the minute movement of my finger.

I repeat this action, going through the process until a profound silence settles over the entire room.

"Do you see that?" Irina asks.

"I do," Chey responds.

I bring myself to tap my finger once more.

"Is it a malfunction, do you think?" Evander asks.

"No. She's doing it," Irina says. "Hello, can you please give me two taps of your finger to confirm that you understand me?"

It's challenging to muster the strength to tap twice. The pain surges through my body, overwhelming my senses. Every nerve is ablaze, and if I could vocalize my agony, it would be deafening. I am depleted, akin to running a relentless marathon without respite.

Tap. Tap.

I did it.

"This is incredible!" Irina says, happiness coating her voice. "Would you be willing to help us? Tap once."

Tap.

Chey interjects with a severe tone. "It could potentially lead to your death if you proceed."

"Tap once if you understand," Irina says.

Tap.

"There's your damn consent, Chey," Irina says. "Your sign."

Chey asks, "Could you please give me two taps if you consent to participate in an experiment that involves the potential removal of your implant?"

Tap. Tap.

I wish they would stop questioning me and focus on their work instead. I'm on the brink of falling asleep, drained of energy. It's as if I've used up several days' worth of mental energy.

"What now?" Evander asks.

"Evander, please stand guard at the door. Nobody must find out about what we are working on. Irina can take detailed notes as I walk through the process." Chey's voice carries authority as she speaks. "I require complete silence unless I specifically instruct or ask for something. I need space to concentrate and work."

"Done," Evander and Irina say in unison.

"First, where do they inject this implant?" Chey asks.

"In the early ones, somewhere around the neck. Newer ones, in their forearm," Irina says.

There's the slight smack of gloves being pulled on, material brushing against my skin, and the soft fabric touching the contours of my neck.

"What is it supposed to feel like?"

"It's about the size of a grain of rice, and you can feel it just beneath the skin," Irina explains.

Chey pushes my hair aside. Her fingertips move up my neck, her touch like a feather grazing my skin. I can feel her curiosity as her fingers explore every contour and ridge. It's tucked away just behind my right ear, a concealed secret. Her movements are deliberate and unhurried. Her touch remains delicate, and she's almost hesitant as if she's afraid of missing the subtlest detail. She moves up to the area behind my right ear and probes, and I can tell by how she lingers and moves the implant back and forth beneath her fingertip that she's found it.

"It's here," Chey says. "I'll administer a local anesthetic to numb the area, then make a small incision to extract it."

As the needle slides into my skin, I feel a brief, intense stinging sensation reminiscent of a bee sting that courses through my entire body. My muscles involuntarily contract, and my body stiffens as if resisting the removal of the implant, almost like the implant itself senses it's being evicted from its home. Then a wave of excruciating pain returns to my brain; it's the worst yet. My body starts convulsing, and my arms tighten against the restraints. This is scary. I don't like it. It's a solid pain. Pain that is indescribable in the worst way possible. The type of pain associated with death.

I realize there may be no escape from this predicament. Today is the final day. Everything around me falls silent. A small trickle of something moves down the back of my neck. I have the urge to wipe it away, but the restraints hold my arms back.

Wait.

Did I move on my own?

Did I really . . . move?

I focus all my attention on the task and mentally instruct my right foot to extend outward. Concentrating, I feel the subtle shift as my right foot follows my mental command.

The burlap sack is still tied around my head, and the texture of the fabric scratches against my skin. A single tear escapes down my cheek. A feeling of liberation is washing over me, as if a heavy burden has been lifted from my shoulders. Overwhelming relief and freedom fills every part of my being, bringing deep joy and gratitude. I never believed this day would come, but here I am, free from the invisible shackles that have held me back.

Amid the rush of emotions, I hear a faint popping sound followed by a *thud*.

"What the hell?" Irina exclaims. "Oh, no, no, no, no."

The disbelief in her voice indicates that something terrible or unexpected occurred.

Evander's voice trembles as he asks, "What happened? Oh my God, what happened?!"

"Wait. Wait. Don't come any closer," Irina says.

"Why not?"

"When Chey removed the implant, it unexpectedly popped. The rupture released a few droplets of an unidentified liquid into the air, and within seconds the mist enveloped her," Irina explains.

"You okay, though?"

"Yeah, I wasn't in the vicinity of the mist."

"Put something over your face," Evander says. "Are there masks?"

"In the drawer over there. There are surgical masks."

I hear Evander's footsteps, followed by the distinct noise of a drawer sliding open.

"Here," Evander says.

I assume they secured the masks over their faces. I also remain untouched by the mist. I recall the doctor explaining this to Paul Randall after my implantation; it was a security protocol aimed at making it challenging, if not impossible, for us to be freed. If those droplets can't enter our nostrils, we will live. The burlap sack over my head has become an indispensable lifeline, shielding me from the toxic mist and potentially saving my life. I'm thankful for its protection in this critical moment.

"Feel her pulse," Irina says.

"She's gone."

"Shit, I don't know how I'll explain this."

"We killed Chey."

"We didn't kill her," Irina insists, her voice trembling as she tries to convince herself as much as the others. "It was Paul Randall. If it weren't her, it would have been someone else."

"That's true," I say. My voice sounds weird and raspy, almost like an old car that hasn't been driven in years.

Their breath catches in their throats. The sack rises from my weary eyes and I stare into two sets of eyes. Irina's features exude a rugged beauty, an aura of toughness I might have found intimidating before the implant. On the other hand, Evander appears to be a clean-cut gentleman with kind eyes and a thick head of brown hair that adds a touch of warmth to his demeanor.

Irina adjusts the restraints on my arms, and within moments the first restraint is undone, followed swiftly by the next.

I refuse to look down at my feet, at Chey—I can't bear to see the cost of my freedom.

A look of relief spreads across Irina's face. "It worked," she said with a smile. "What's your name?"

"Kinley."

"Nice to meet you, Kinley. How do you feel?"

"Weird?"

Irina nods. "I'd imagine so. Would you be open to joining Evander and me in a counseling session with the leader, Rebecca, here? You'd soften the blow over the loss of Chey if we could prove that the implants can be removed."

"I was one of the first. I don't know if that makes a difference. There aren't many like me," I explain. "The others are different. It was an experiment. They didn't proceed with more than a dozen more implants like mine. The rest are not made of the same material or in the same place, as you seem to be aware. The other implants are more difficult to remove, designed with more complex mechanisms for attachment.

I overheard them discussing it while I was Implanted. They don't realize we remain aware despite our lack of control."

"Does every type of implant have the mist?" Irina inquires.

"I'm not entirely certain." I hesitate, addressing Irina before turning to Evander. "We need to acquire the procedures. If I recall correctly, they should be on the city's East side. I remember overhearing discussions within the Sons of Paul. They can access the information."

Irina tilts her head to the side and asks, "So you were conscious while Implanted? The entire time? Is there anything else I should know?"

"There's this document. It's called Eden Falling, an entire outline of my implant and others. Paul Randall has specific procedures for constructing the implants, as well as guidelines for their removal. He's even outlined a procedure in the event that a group, such as your team, learns how to remove the implants. It's all in Eden Falling."

Irina's smile widens. "You will be even more valuable than I had anticipated."

THE SONS OF PAUL

NEV

The musty scent of sweaty socks lingered in the abandoned high school locker room. The Sons of Paul gathered in the renovated inner-city school, a project initiated by Paul Randall. Nev speculated that it might have been a private school because of its size and location in the East district. However, such details were of no concern to him then or now.

The pristine white suit lay across one of the light-brown benches. It was adorned with an intricately designed dove and a remarkably conspicuous vine. The emblem symbolized the idea that Paul Randall was the central figure and the Sons of Paul and the Implanted were interconnected branches stemming from him. Nev couldn't help but roll his eyes.

His parents had persuaded him to join the Sons of Paul, emphasizing the immense respect associated with the duty. However, his parents failed to mention or consider the reality of the limited number of un-Implanted individuals. The Implanted only consisted of the middle and lower classes, while the elites—comprising politicians, rulers, and the upper echelons—remained un-Implanted. Paul Randall, his boss, considered the lower classes the most unsophisticated and criminally corrupt, hence the grand idea for the mandated implants.

Nev's fingertips glided over the supple material in its flattened state. He paused, taking a deep breath before embracing his role of enforcer against the Implanted. His job was to diminish the ranks and resources of the rebels. It had become increasingly clear there were more rebels in clandestine hiding than Paul Randall or anyone had dared to imagine. The mandate hadn't unfolded as well as originally intended. A wry smile graced Nev's lips as he contemplated the resilience of these elusive rebels, people who were inevitably aligned against him now.

The Sons of Paul faced a growing challenge. The rebel forces continued to capture more and more Implanted individuals, weakening the organization and posing a significant threat to Paul Randall's regime and his efforts to maintain control. This had prompted an urgent need to recruit more people to join the Sons of Paul and support their mission.

Nev slid the uniform over his head, allowing the weight of the heavy material to settle over him. He secured a crisp white vest with the same ridiculous emblem and cinched it with a white belt. This attire symbolized commitment to a role he didn't want, but that his parents insisted on. Supporting someone as morally corrupt as Paul Randall made Nev's skin prickle, and he wondered whether he truly knew his parents. Nev knew his family's social standing shielded him from the realities the Implanted and the rebels and their families faced, and while he remained grateful, it made him sick.

The locker room door let out a high-pitched creak as it swung open. George stood at the far end of the locker room, surrounded by rows of gray lockers.

"My man!" George strolled over and slapped him on the shoulder. "Look at you! It's about time you joined the ranks."

Nev strained a smile at his friend. George's face hadn't changed since their youth. The same angular bone structure, prominent brow, and mouth reminded Nev of a displeased professor.

"Yeah. It's about time."

George took in Nev's vest, then reached out to adjust its positioning. "Remember, when you encounter a rebel, act without hesitation."

"What's the likelihood of seeing a rebel?"

"It depends on where they have us today. Regardless, they've been out more lately, with more confidence than usual," George said, smiling, the freckles clustering in his dimples. "I can't wait for you to take one out."

"And what do we do if we don't see one?"

George shrugged. "Maybe push around an Implanted."

Nev's eyes narrowed. "What?"

"They can't think anyway."

"How do you know?"

"I don't, but who cares."

Nev shook his head. He disagreed with George, his parents, Paul Randall—the entire civilization supporting this. "I do."

George laughed, raising a blond eyebrow. "Seriously?"

Nev sighed. There was no sense in discussing matters further. "So, what first?"

"Well, you'll be in my unit—that's all you need to know." George turned and walked, expecting Nev to follow, then stopped and said over his shoulder, "Andrew is the big guy. He'll have our duty station for the week."

Nev followed George down the impeccably clean, brightly lit hallway. The polished gray tiles reflected the overhead lights. Nev stared at the back of George's close-cropped blond hair as the white walls closed in on them. With every step taking them closer to the rest of the unit, Nev's stomach turned sour. He wondered whether their duty station would be in the calm and peaceful East district, where not much ever happened, or to an area where the rebels carried out attacks against the Sons of Paul. The South and West districts remained under rebel control, at least as far as Nev had gathered from the whispers circulating this side of the city.

The hallway led to a spacious room with walls painted a muted shade of gray. The six men, all wearing identical white attire, glanced at them as they entered.

They greeted George while scrutinizing Nev's uniform from head to toe, taking in every inch and detail for any signs of disarray or incorrect placement.

Although these men would watch his six, they shared no friendship. No, not in the slightest. Their responsibility remained dedicated to Paul Randall and Arkin, not to one another. If shot today, these men wouldn't shed a tear for Nev. They'd go about their day. The harsh realities of this life were evident, though undisclosed.

"Hey everyone, I want you to meet Nev," George announced with a grin. "He's an old friend, so go easy on him, alright?"

George's eyes, a mesmerizing deep blue, fixed on Nev before glancing back at the group. There was a big man at the head of the group. *That must be Andrew.*

Andrew handed George a cream-colored envelope, which he tucked into his pocket.

"We're to be in the Southwest today," said Andrew as he stepped forward.

Great. The most dangerous locations combined.

Andrew's imposing height and bright orange hair made him stand out. He reminded Nev of a lumberjack.

George wrinkled his freckled nose. "Southwest is the filthiest."

"At least we'll have something to do," one of the other men said.

"Ha! John, the truth-teller. More Implanted, more rebels, more chaos. Let's go, boys." George's grin stretched across his face, lacking any genuine warmth. The smile faded when the other men fell into a disciplined line, quickly replaced by a serious expression as he locked onto Nev again. "You're about to experience a challenging first week. If you can push through this, you'll be able to tackle anything that comes your way."

Nev pushed his black hair out of his eyes. "If you say so."

"Stick with Andrew," George said. "He'll keep you alive."

George walked alongside the unit formation of the Sons of Paul. When he reached the front of the line, he clapped, prompting the soldiers to follow him through a side entrance. They emerged outside to find a white military vehicle adorned with the identical emblem as their uniforms awaiting their arrival.

As the men filed into the vehicle's enclosed body, George strolled over to Nev. "You'll be on the exterior, holding onto the back with Andrew."

Nev glanced at Andrew, who nodded.

"Okay," Nev said.

"Make sure to stay alert, and watch out for anything important we might need to stop for," George said. "You'll learn a lot from Andrew."

"All the while being shot at," Nev said, remembering the stories of the Sons of Paul being swarmed outside their vehicles by bands of rebels. Nev's hands trembled as a wave of anxiety surged through his body. His fingers curled into tight fists as he tried to conceal the tension in his muscles, and the fear creeping up.

"Maybe." George shrugged. "Recall my previous words: do not hesitate, take action."

Nev's shoulders sank as he averted his gaze from George. He hoisted himself onto the cramped right side of the vehicle. Joining the Sons of Paul weighed heavily on him, and the tight space only amplified his discomfort.

"Boy," Andrew said. "Your feet. Secure them under the groove."

Nev noticed a nook that seemed to be a perfect fit for his boots. "Thank you," he said, sliding his feet in, dangling but firmly anchored.

Andrew inclined his head and looked ahead.

Nev released a deep sigh, resignation enveloping him. He shifted his weight to mirror Andrew's posture, realizing the opportunity to glean significant insights from the mannerisms and nonverbal cues of his superiors.

The vehicle's engine roared to life. Nev gripped the cool metal bar beside him as the vehicle surged forward with a jerk, filling the air with its powerful hum. Along the road, they passed people who waved at them, and some women appeared to take pleasure in showering them with attention.

As they sped down the paved streets, Nev was forced to grip the bar so tightly he feared his hands would lose circulation. He couldn't shake the sensation that a strong gust of wind could send him flying backward like a makeshift parachute into the sky.

As they journeyed further from the East, the ride became progressively bumpier. Abandoned cars scattered along the road were reminders of the mass exodus that occurred over a year ago, when government-enforced mandates took effect. Why hadn't Paul Randall cleared the streets of these obstacles, Nev wondered. Probably to impede any potential escape attempts.

A long time had passed since Nev ventured to this part of the city. The stark difference between the East and the Southwest took him aback. The East had fresh, crisp air and looked surreal in the sunlight, with gleaming surfaces that seemed to sparkle. However, the Southwest was a dramatic departure: heavy, acrid fumes suffocated the senses, and the buildings, streets, and overall landscape were cloaked in weathered shades of brown that bore an air of neglect and decay.

The Southwest district teemed with the Implanted. Their movements were eerily precise, almost robotic, and their eyes were devoid of life or emotion, exuding a haunting emptiness.

Nev had often heard whispers about the Implanted, but coming face-to-face with them was an entirely different and disturbing experience. He struggled to comprehend the full extent of what had befallen them. The Implanted appeared almost artificial; their very existence defied understanding. Nev couldn't shake the profound sickness that settled over him as he confronted the harsh reality of a working class reduced to little more than flesh-and-blood machines.

The consequences of this advanced technology burdened Nev, and he'd begun to question how any political leader or individual could endorse such a dehumanizing practice. He felt disillusioned with his parents, and an unidentifiable feeling now replaced his idealized image of them. Meanwhile, Paul Randall was determined to broaden the influence of the Implanted business, envisioning a global expansion with himself at the helm, the mastermind orchestrating it all.

Nev stood frozen in place, seeking any sign of recognition in the cold gazes of the people around him, but none could be found. As the vehicle inched forward, his gaze shifted to the faces around him, no longer searching for signs of life but for any semblance of familiarity. He studied the multitude of Implanted, noting the diverse ages and genders, yet not a single person seemed familiar.

Until *her*.

The air was still as he caught sight of her. She stood there, small in stature but exuding a quiet strength, with flawless skin and intricately braided dark brown hair. He remembered her long, untamed hair cascading down her back, how it had often distracted him from schoolwork whenever he was seated behind her.

Irina.

From elementary through high school, Irina was a classmate from a middle-class background. She was Implanted.

Despite being from a lower socioeconomic background, Irina had always excelled in her studies, displaying exceptional talent and unwavering dedication. Her mother had utilized her connections to ensure Irina and her brother gained admission to the top educational institutions in the city, offering her the best possible education.

Irina was Implanted.

Once a vibrant, independent, and empathetic individual with a contagious smile, Irina was devoid of her former personality, appearing lifeless. It was evident that the implant was responsible for this drastic transformation.

Andrew's fists pounded three times against the back of the vehicle, jolting Nev out of his trance. "Stop!"

As the vehicle came to a stop, Andrew leaped from the back and marched past Nev without uttering a single word. Andrew's determined strides led him straight toward Irina, who was oblivious to his approach.

The sound of gunshots tore through the air. An explosion reverberated nearby, shaking the ground. The vehicle's back doors burst open, and the rest of the unit tumbled out, throwing Nev to the ground.

His head collided with something solid, and darkness crept into his field of vision. With George's help, he managed to pull himself up and stumble behind a concrete wall. The taste of copper filled his mouth.

"What's going on?"

"The rebels," George said between gritted teeth. "Get your gun."

Nev pulled the gun over his shoulder. "Irina . . ."

"Irina is the problem!"

"She's Implanted!"

"She's a rebel!"

The air was filled with another loud bang. They pressed their backs against the cold, unforgiving concrete. Their once pristine uniforms, marked with stains and covered in soot, now blended in with the dark surroundings.

"I just saw her," Nev said. "She's Implanted."

"It's a facade. She's the mastermind behind most of the rebel's missions."

"Not Irina."

George withdrew the envelope from his vest and shoved it at Nev's chest. "Go on, take a look for yourself."

Nev ripped the envelope open as George popped his head over the concrete barrier and returned fire. Inside, Nev found a blurry photograph of Irina accompanied by a detailed list of her actions and a letter addressed to George, signed by Paul

Randall, describing that she would face the consequences for her actions.

"I don't believe it," Nev said.

"Nev, we're here because of *her*," George said, carefully peering over the barrier and firing a few more rounds.

Nev scanned the surrounding area, his eyes sweeping every nook and cranny. Despite his thorough search, there was no trace of any Implanted individuals. They had vanished without a trace, leaving a sense of eerie emptiness. He reminded himself they were designed to flee when chaos erupted, which was a silver lining amid the confusion.

Nev tucked the envelope into the deep recesses of his pocket, choosing not to return it to George, who was engrossed in return fire. A stealthy group of rebels were peering out from windows and positioned along rooftops. Nev opted not to confront them directly. Instead, he fired a shot into the general area, all the while attempting to locate Irina and discern her activities.

A bullet flew by his head.

Nev's heart pounded like a drum, the adrenaline coursing through his veins. His hands trembled as George grasped him by the vest, pulling him away from the concrete barrier and the devastating scene beyond. Nev struggled to keep up with George's swift movements, stumbling over scattered debris as they hurried away from the chaos.

As they rounded the corner of a building, the butt of a gun slammed into George's face. The crunching sound was one of the worst things Nev had ever heard. He reached for his gun in defense, unable to do anything for George, who was sprawled on the pavement, hopefully just unconscious.

Nev and those familiar dark green eyes engaged in a wordless standoff, their gazes fixed on each other with unspoken intensity, guns trained and ready.

"Nev."

"Irina."

"Fancy seeing you here and on opposite sides, unfortunately for you."

Despite the overwhelming desire to lower the weapon, Nev struggled. He couldn't help but notice Irina's braided hair, a clear indicator of her preparedness for battle, and the piercing in her eyebrow. As much as he wanted to trust her, lingering doubt refused to leave Nev's mind, knowing they were on opposite sides of the conflict.

"I don't want to hurt you, Irina."

She wore a pensive look, her head tilted to the side ever so slightly. "You wouldn't do that, Nev."

"What makes you so sure?"

"We have history."

Nev felt a lump forming in his throat. He swallowed hard, struggling to contain the surge of emotion welling up inside him. George was still lying sprawled on the ground, but it was Andrew's condition that truly alarmed him—he appeared to be in a much worse state, lying there next to George.

"I will if I have to."

Irina clicked her tongue. "If you had the guts to do it, you would have already. Just like I did without hesitation when dealing with George and whoever *that* is."

Nev couldn't tear his eyes away from George, who lay motionless and unconscious on the cold, hard ground, his chest rising and falling faintly with each breath.

"What do you want?" Nev finally said.

Irina placed her hand on the metal of the weapon's barrel and exerted gentle pressure to lower it. "That's much better," she remarked, flashing a self-assured smile. "Let's create some distance between us and your friend," she said, frowning as she looked disdainfully down at George's body, "in case he happens to regain consciousness."

The narrow alley provided a brief respite from the gunfire and turmoil unfolding. Irina guided him deeper into the alley, and with each step, it felt as though they were entering the calm center of a storm, where the unrest outside harmonized into a precarious symphony of threats.

"I want your help," she said, coming to a stop, her voice filled with urgency.

"Help? How?"

"I need intel."

"What intel?"

"Details about the implants and instructions on how to disarm them. I believe the document is called Eden Falling. Any information of a similar nature is also valuable."

"Eden Falling . . ." Nev shook his head. "I can't."

Irina's head tilted. "Are you trying to tell me that you enjoy being a part of that fascist group? I thought I knew you better, Nev."

Nev's lips tightened into a thin, straight line. A palpable constriction gripped his throat, and with a tinge of concern, he asked, "What are your plans?"

"To restore the world to its previous state. To halt the progression of the Implanted."

"It's impossible."

Irina glanced over her shoulder toward the destruction unfolding outside the alleyway. "It's not," she said. "Do you know what's happening out here, Nev? People like me, on the other side, are being pursued and forcibly implanted. I don't have your privilege or wealth. The only path left for me is resistance. Striving for change."

Nev took a step back, reflecting on their robotic appearance, the emotions that being on this side evoked in him, and the deep sorrow he felt for Irina and those in her situation. "Where is your family?"

"Implanted."

"I don't . . . understand . . ."

"What's not to understand? My mom pulled strings to get me in the school you and George attended, but I'm not one of you." She advanced toward him. "Living in your lavish penthouse on the affluent East side, reaping the benefits of your parents' accomplishments. You've never experienced the fear of the implants, the agony of losing loved ones to it, the struggle to bring them back," she said, clear contempt in her voice. "Nev, you have no idea what it's like to endure hunger, thirst, or despair. You've never had to."

Nev was unable to look Irina in the eyes, consumed by shame. He had always esteemed Irina and held her in high regard. He lowered his head and rubbed his eyes.

"Where would I even begin?" he said.

Irina let out a deep sigh. "You see or hear about Eden Falling, you share that with me. The issue I'm grappling with is that the implant can't be removed without the proper procedure, and that document has it."

Nev swept his dark hair out of his eyes, glancing down the alley to confirm that George was still unconscious. "What happens if I get caught?"

"The rebels will come to rescue you before anything can happen," Irina assured him.

Nev gazed at her. Her green eyes were so captivating and she knew it. "Okay. I'll help."

Irina's smile was genuine, reaching the corners of her eyes and brightening the creases. "Okay. When you have the information, flip your bedroom light on and off four times quickly," Irina instructed. "Then we can meet at the coffee shop. Remember? Espresso-self."

Nev smiled, recalling the memories from their weekend meet-ups. Irina was the kind of person everyone wanted to be around; she was a devout friend who made everyone laugh. A small group of them used to meet at Espresso-self on Saturday mornings. "I remember. What if you miss the lights?"

Irina's smile was warm and reassuring as she spoke. "I'm always watching, but I suggest doing it around ten p.m. Things are typically calmer then, and it's easier to navigate. We'll meet the following morning."

The sound of gunfire filled every inch of the space with a relentless barrage of bullets. He cast a furtive glance over his shoulder at George, aware that any movement from him could trigger an alert or prompt the unit to embark in pursuit through the surrounding area. After a tense moment, he cautiously uttered a word that sealed his fate.

"Deal."

"Good. Give me your gun."

"Why?"

"So you're not suspected."

"Okay." Nev was unsure of Irina's intentions but handed over the gun.

"Once again, thank you, Nev," she said with a grim expression. She thrust the butt of the gun into his face, and everything went black.

* * *

Two weeks had passed since the encounter with Irina. The sharp, throbbing pain across the bridge of Nev's nose was a constant reminder of their agreement. Despite the discomfort, he felt relief that no one appeared aware of what had happened.

Nev dedicated himself to acquiring information within the Sons of Paul. He showed unwavering commitment by participating in meetings so that he could understand the organization's plans, intricate schemes, and the complex world of the Implanted.

Nev found it effortless to become involved in the workings of the Sons of Paul. Paul Randall, the leader, sought out and welcomed enthusiastic young men who admired and praised him. After the devastating attack that led to the loss of most of the unit, the survivors were presented and pushed into yet more meetings, giving them a reprieve from fighting until more recruits could be gathered to refill their unit.

Even though Paul Randall never physically attended, information about his whereabouts was hard to come by. Instead, his presence was represented on a screen at the head of the table. Due to concerns for safety amid rebel attacks and his general distrust of others, he relied solely on private security. However, Nev's participation provided a valuable opportunity to learn from and earn the trust of high-ranking officials who shared important information and documents.

Soon Nev found himself in charge of thoroughly reviewing the documents' contents before each delivery, but even as a go-between, he almost always came up empty-handed regarding useful information for Irina. On this occasion, however, as Nev was leaving a meeting, one of the higher-ups handed him a document to deliver. This time, Nev was surprised to find himself in possession of a document containing crucial information that could greatly benefit Irina.

Eden Falling. A new draft. What were the odds?

The document provided detailed insights into the implants, covering the evolution from the initial version to the latest upcoming models intended for use on rebels captured and sold to various parts of the world. It delved into the materials involved in the procedure and even touched upon the toxic substances. There was so much information, even a plan of what to do if the rebels started to gain the upper hand. Nev was astonished at his good fortune. He had to get this information to Irina, and fast. Still, he was also responsible for delivering it to Paul Randall's secretary in the next twenty minutes.

There was only one thing he could do: make a copy.

Nev paused to calm his nerves as he made his way to the copier, greeting people with nods and smiles, trying to appear friendly and approachable, like he was supposed to be there. No one seemed to suspect anything. When he finally reached the rarely visited copy room, he felt relieved knowing he wouldn't be disturbed. The room smelled musty, and the copier was an old-fashioned cream color.

He slid the stack of papers into the feeder and punched in a sequence of buttons. His eyes followed the smooth, synchronized movement of the pages as the forbidden copy was made. After dutifully returning the original document to its folder, he concealed the copy beneath his vest, just as the door creaked open. In that heart-stopping moment, Nev's pulse raced and his stomach plummeted. He gingerly turned to avoid arousing suspicion, forcing himself to maintain composure.

"Nev, what are you doing in here?" George asked.

Nev stifled his gasp and turned to give George a reassuring smile. "I was just making sure the copier was working. I've been sent back to make copies before, and there are days when the copier malfunctions. I just wanted to save time and ensure everything was ready in case they requested copies."

"Sure," George replied. "Have you come across anything interesting?"

Nev shrugged. "I wouldn't know."

George stood with his arms crossed, a skeptical look on his face. "Are you seriously telling me you never even sneaked a peek outside of these meetings?"

Nev chuckled. "George, you've known me since I was four. Does that align with my by-the-book personality?"

George burst into laughter. "I should have known."

Nev shrugged. "You should have."

"Let me see the document then?"

Nev held the document over his head, eyes wide. "Are you out of your mind? They'd skin me alive if I shared this information."

"They won't know. Plus, they already covered some of it in the meeting."

"Some of it, George," Nev said. George's once-straight nose now sat crooked on his face, a lingering reminder of the day Irina broke it. Thankfully, Nev's nose was only sore.

George gazed at Nev's vest and shook his head. "You should learn how to put that thing on properly, Nev. I can't always be the one fixing it for you."

Nev looked down at his vest and pretended to shrug it off, attempting to stifle his mounting panic. "I need to pay better attention, that's all."

He silently prayed that the papers wouldn't fall out or attract George's attention.

George nodded. "There's a meeting with Mr. Randall scheduled for tomorrow morning. We must arrive on time."

"Of course," Nev replied, nodding as George straightened the vest. "Perhaps we can regroup afterward?"

"Of course. But make sure to wear your vest correctly tomorrow. Fasten the buckles on the sides and adjust it so that it fits snugly on your shoulders."

"You got it," Nev said. "I'll catch you in the morning."

That night Nev alerted the rebels, praying Irina would see his signal.

* * *

In the quiet, pre-dawn hours, Nev slipped into Arkin's empty streets. Despite the substantial distance to Espresso-self, he was convinced he could deliver Eden Falling to Irina and keep his appointment with Paul Randall. He treaded through the dimly lit cityscape, mulling over the possibility of Paul appearing in person, though based on past encounters, it seemed unlikely. When he arrived at Espresso-self, the desolate scene before him struck a chord of dismay in his heart. The once-thriving and vibrant coffee shop had been replaced by an unsettling shroud of neglect, dust, and scattered refuse.

As he pressed open the creaky front door, he was met with the lingering aroma of old ground beans. He searched for any sign of Irina, but found only a scattering of empty coffee cups and mugs strewn across the floor. The yawning entrance to the basement called out to him, and he proceeded down the weathered steps. The atmosphere grew heavy with the smell of moist earth that wrapped around him as he ventured deeper into the poorly illuminated expanse.

"You made it," Irina said.

Nev whipped around at her approach. "I did," he said, reaching under the vest. "This should help. At least, I hope it does."

Irina accepted the document from him. She skimmed through the pages, then tucked it in her backpack. "Eden Falling. I knew I could count on you. Thank you. This changes everything."

"So, it'll help? It's what you were looking for?"

"More than that," she said, smiling. "There's something important I have to tell you, a word of caution."

"Caution?"

Irina shook her head, suspicion in her eyes. "A warning."

"Like what?"

"I don't know, but I have a feeling. It would be best if you came with me. Don't go back."

Nev wrinkled his forehead. "Irina, I can't just vanish. I can't leave my parents behind. If I abandon the Sons of Paul, what will happen to them? Paul Randall doesn't take these things lightly."

Her sigh conveyed worry and concern. "I believe you've been discovered. There are individuals within The Shield, the organization I belong to, who secretly monitor the Sons of Paul. Rumor has it that there's been a betrayal from within. If you're accused of being a traitor, it will be extremely dire for your parents. We'll do our best to get them out."

"They'll never accept help from the . . ."

"From people lesser than them?" Irina said.

Nev paused. He took a hesitant step backward, his eyes betraying his inner conflict. "I'll need to persuade them on my own."

Irina nodded. "I understand."

"I'll meet you here. In a few hours?"

She slung her backpack over her shoulder. "I'll be here."

* * *

Nev didn't linger for too long before returning to the East district. The return journey from Espresso-self seemed to drag on longer than the initial trip, primarily because certain Sons of Paul units had begun their shift. The meeting with Paul Randall was soon, but he had enough time for a quick detour to visit his parents. Although it was only five minutes from today's meeting place, he unexpectedly crossed paths with George as he turned the corner of the imposing skyscraper.

George flashed him a lopsided grin. "Where are you off to? The meeting is in that direction."

"I need to talk to my parents."

"There's no time for that. Paul Randall is meeting us, in person."

Nev felt George's powerful grip on his shoulder as he was spun around.

As he and George walked together to the meeting location, Nev grappled with the impossibility of his situation. There was no escaping this—he would have to head straight to his parents' place after, but the daunting prospect of trying to sway them clouded his thoughts. A palpable sense of peril made him feel as if danger lurked in every shadow. He held his breath, feeling the weight of the impending confrontation closing in on him.

They entered a conference room with a long, gleaming table and a wide window offering a stunning view of the city. Nev and George, members of the Sons of Paul, stood—as was customary during in-person meetings with Paul Randall, which were rare. Sitting was a rare privilege for them.

"He should be here anytime now," George said.

A few moments later, the door creaked open and Paul Randall walked in. Nev straightened up and reached out to shake his hand.

Paul Randall stood at an impressive height, his brown hair neatly slicked back. He had a commanding presence that demanded respect and admiration.

"Good morning, Sons of Paul," Paul Randall said.

"Good morning, Mr. Randall," Nev and George said.

"I hear you deliver my documents, Nev. I appreciate that more than you know."

"I'm happy to help," Nev said.

Paul Randall's lips curled into a smile. His gaze shifted between George and Nev, anticipation lingering in the air.

"Where were you this morning, Nev?"

Nev tried to keep himself steady. "In my room."

"You were going to your parents," George said.

Nev's heart fluttered in warning as he confessed. "I was."

Paul Randall clicked his tongue and didn't look away. "Have you been to the copier recently?"

"He was there yesterday," George offered. "He makes copies of the documents sometimes."

"For what?" Paul asked.

Nev stood still, aware that he had been discovered.

"For context, the copier room has cameras. Small cameras, but cameras nonetheless. You are not the first traitor in my ranks," Paul Randall said, leveling Nev with a look. "And you," he turned to George, "were too blinded to see the documents under his vest!"

George flinched.

"Where is the other copy, Nev?" Paul Randall asked, the authority in his voice commanding Nev to reveal his secrets.

Nev remained still, not a muscle twitching or a word escaping his lips.

THE CODE OF HOPE

Paul Randall's smile twisted into a sinister expression of satisfaction. "Cat got your tongue?"

George moved ahead. "Mr. Randall, I'm certain there is a logical explanation for this."

Paul Randall cast a quick, commanding glance at George and said, "Arrest him."

"Sir?"

"It's either you or him."

George turned to Nev, his mouth agape.

"It's okay," Nev whispered.

George grabbed Nev's hands and pinned them behind his back.

"Lock him up. He'll be tried as a traitor," Paul Randall said.

THE VINE

PAUL RANDALL

Ever since I was young, I've been haunted by a pervasive sense of fear. It's the kind of fear that stems from the uncertainties of life, the looming specter of failure, the relentless pressure to live up to others' expectations. This fear has a tight grip on me, guiding every decision I make.

As the leader of Arkin, I find myself wrestling with the same anxieties that plagued me during my childhood. This underlying fear has always been a part of me, perhaps stemming from my earliest experiences. It could also be due to my mother's unfounded fears and her belief that even the slightest mishap could have catastrophic consequences.

I stand by the window, peering at the city I govern. The gleaming metropolis appears pristine, beautiful, secure. It's almost like observing a flawless masterpiece handcrafted by the most fastidious artist. I've realized that although an ever-present fear continues to push me toward my goals, the overwhelming desire for control in all its forms is what truly consumes me.

"Mr. Randall, it's time."

I pivot on my heel and adorn my face with a warm, inviting smile. This smile is my trademark, an emblem of my influence and control. Through this expression, I project an image of kindness and charm, instilling confidence in my followers as a trustworthy and captivating leader.

"Thank you, Lisa," I say, my hand gliding down the front of my gray suit. "It's hard to fathom that weeks have slipped by since the boy's treachery."

Today, Nev will be sentenced and punished for the charges against him. The final decision has been made, regardless of any opposing views. It has been determined that he is guilty. He will be strung up. I haven't decided where, but his arms will feel like they're being ripped from their sockets. A traitor's punishment. A rebel's fate.

Lisa's smile lacks the warmth that usually reaches her eyes. There is a faint smudge of pink lipstick on one of her front teeth. Although her lips are thin, she tries to give the impression of fuller lips by overlining them. Her clenched jaw indicates tension and forcedness. I'll need to pay close attention to her.

"Yes. Hard to believe," Lisa says.

I should have assumed there would be people disconcerted about Nev, like Lisa here. He is admired for his intelligence and likability, which could benefit Arkin's expansion into new territories. Lisa and Nev had established a pleasant and amicable relationship during his visits to deliver documents. However, he is a traitor and will soon face the consequences.

Despite my initial expectations, Irina did not attempt to rescue Nev. I saw Nev as potential bait, assuming the opportunity to rescue him would be too tempting and lead to her capture. If I could capture Irina, the rebels would flounder. Although she's not their leader, her influence is paramount. Nevertheless, her hesitancy to make a move demonstrates a deep understanding of the risks and of her strategic position. She's a cunning and shrewd individual, and her astuteness is commendable.

As I make my way to the door, my heart quickens. Just as I'm about to leave, a weight in my stomach prompts me to utter, "Oh, and Lisa."

"Yes, sir?" Lisa peers at me over her square-framed glasses.

"We do not mourn traitors; otherwise, how shall I know if you are not one yourself?" Her expression contorts in terror upon hearing these words. Despite the apprehension creeping over her, I maintain a disarming smile, leaving her to contend with her fears. If I must endure the unease, it is only fair that she confronts it, too. Let the dread consume her.

My ebony shoes emit a crisp squeak as I move along the spotless corridor, which smells like fresh Clorox. The immaculate floors seem to shimmer under the illumination. A smile forms on my face as I bask in the contentment of being surrounded by such a neat and organized setting. A comforting cocoon.

As I turn the corner, the solemn courtroom comes into view. A faint scent of dust and mothballs lingers in the air, but the sharp smell of Clorox cuts through it. Nev is standing alone at the front, exposed to everyone as the traitor he is. His mother struggles to hold back tears while his father's face remains stoic.

I intend to assemble a team of guards to keep a watchful eye on them, in case they rebel. George, a friend of Nev's, could be open to helping out. Family members can sometimes be a potential weakness. I'm thankful I don't possess any vulnerabilities that could be exploited against me.

Judge Lance, a longtime friend, strides to the gleaming mahogany podium, places the folder on its polished surface, and extracts the document from the pile. It's the same document I handed over earlier in the day detailing my upcoming sentencing. Lance's demeanor almost mirrors that of a reverent pastor. I look at Nev, who exudes confidence. He stands tall, head held high with an unwavering focus fixed on me. It's as if he sees right through me. My heart races and my stomach twists into knots.

He can't reach you, Paul, I silently reassure myself.

Lance flips through the document with his sausage-fat fingers. He has a stout build, with sparse hair and a round face. Despite his lack of physical intimidation, he exudes an air of authority befitting his position. Rather than sitting as usual, I position myself at the back of the room to gain a different perspective on the sentencing. Standing in the last row, I straighten my spine, recalling my mother's advice: "Don't slouch, Paul. You'll look like a banana by the time you're thirty."

Nev's hair is unkempt, his face hollow, and his skin bears the marks of dirt and filth. Despite his noticeable transformation, a fiery intensity burns in his eyes.

"Sir."

I glance in George's direction, but it's a subtle enough movement to signal that I am aware of his presence.

"George," I acknowledge. I lower my voice and continue, "I have a proposition for you."

Nev watches us like a hawk fixated on its prey. His dark eyes bore into me.

"Anything, sir," George says, his voice trembling. He's anxious about the situation. He's caught in a difficult position—a friend to the traitor yet loyal to the Sons of Paul. I know from rumors that George behaves like a bully rather than showing true bravery, so there's no need to worry too much. Still, if he agrees to this offer, at least his and Nev's parents could be apprehended together if they act out.

"Keep an eye on his parents. I have concerns about how they may respond."

George nods, his expression resolute. "Consider it done. Is there anything else you need from me?"

I meet his gaze as I fully turn toward him. "You assist in delivering the decisive blow."

George's demeanor shifts, a crease forming between his eyebrows as he shakes his head. "I can't."

"That's an order. You'll string him up over one of the streetlights," I say.

Anyone who knows about rebel punishments knows the streetlights are the worst. It's slow and every tug adds further stress, strain, and soreness to the body.

George's lips part as if he's about to speak, but then they press back together in a clear sign of objection.

I clear my throat, feeling the weight of my words. "It's your moment of glory. You will rise from the Sons of Paul to join me as one of my closest councils."

"You're killing him over papers."

I lay my hand on George's shoulder, feeling the taut strength of the muscles beneath my touch. "Those papers, George, were not just any documents. They held crucial information about the implant. If they fall into the wrong hands, our world as we know it could crumble." I meet his gaze, trying to convey the seriousness of the situation. "And, George, to be clear, I have never taken a life, and I cannot bear the burden of blood on my hands. That responsibility falls on you."

"I thought he'd just be . . . implanted?"

"So you can give orders to your unit to rough him up?" I suppress a laugh. "As you do to the Implanted when you have nothing better to do?"

George's eyebrows shoot up to the middle of his forehead. "I wouldn't."

I shrug. "You have to others. Anyway, implantation isn't a viable option for individuals like Nev."

George's thick brows lower as if he's mulling over my words. "It was suitable for worse people than Nev. He isn't a bad guy. Just misled."

"During the early stages of my governance, there was mercy. Traitors like Nev do not deserve mercy or life. The missing document was nowhere to be found. Thanks to your friend, I suspect it has fallen into the hands of our enemies." I raise an eyebrow in suspicion, realizing that I am being put to the test. "In that case, you will execute Nev's punishment at Intersection 7, and be prepared to do the same to your parents."

George's complexion turns pale as he reluctantly agrees. "Fine. I'll do it. Leave my parents out of it, please."

My eyes leave George's childlike face and return to Nev, who's receiving his final sentence.

"Mr. Nev Hurter, how do you plead to the treason charges for allegedly handing over sensitive documents to the rebels?" Judge Lance asks.

Usually, traitors maintain their innocence. I expect him to resist and show emotion, but to my surprise, he remains motionless, turns his head toward me, and confidently confesses, "Guilty."

"Guilty," Judge Lance repeats.

"Now, go retrieve your prisoner, George," I say, clenching my jaw.

George steps forward, his pristine white uniform strikingly juxtaposing Nev's discolored attire.

George guides Nev down the three imposing steps, gripping Nev's upper arm. Despite the tension in Nev's jaw, he manages a small, reassuring smile for his mother as they make their way down the cramped row. As they reach the back doors, Nev's gaze meets mine, conveying many unspoken emotions.

"Anything to say, boy?"

Nev scowls and looks straight ahead.

George leads Nev away, his silence emphasizing the gravity of our situation. I picture him being strung up at Intersection 7, left in the relentless noonday sun. It's a place devoid of mercy, where fate is sealed, and the scavenger birds await their grim feast. I look forward to seeing him suffer. Turning away, I snap my fingers, signaling two members of the Sons of Paul positioned across the room.

"You, go with them," I say to the one on the left, and then to the other, "and you, stay with his family until George returns."

The soldiers march to their command stations. One approaches Nev's family, his mother and father, who are in agreement with whatever the guard says. However, his father's expression changes when his dark eyes shift to me. His mouth tightens. Eventually, he gives me a curt nod.

"Good morning, Mrs. Hurter," I say. She's dressed in a somber black outfit that flows down to her ankles, hinting at the emotional turmoil she will face within the next twenty-four hours, and her inky-black hair is pulled back in a tight bun.

"Morning, Mr. Randall," she says, averting her gaze.

Mr. Hurter looks toward me, his penetrating black eyes locking onto mine. "Paul," he says in a firm, resolute voice.

"Mr. Randall," I correct.

"Mr. Randall," he says, trying to control his features.

I watch Nev's parents be escorted from the room, leaving behind Judge Lance, myself, and a member of the Sons of Paul standing by the side door. I take a deep breath, feeling the weight of the moment, then slip my hands into my pockets as I make my way over to Judge Lance.

He looks up from the folder. "It's done."

"Without a doubt. This course of action may succeed in conveying a message," I say.

"Or it'll anger the rebels, and they'll retaliate."

I let out a chuckle. "They've had plenty of time to try to release him."

"The rebels might have taken advantage of the situation, but considering Irina's involvement, they may have seen it as a possible trap."

"Perhaps."

Lance lets out a heavy sigh. "Paul, we need to put an end to this."

"What?"

Lance's hands rest on the podium, and he takes a moment to collect his thoughts before finally speaking. "This."

I shake my head. "What's the problem, Lance?"

Lance closes the folder. "Upon reflection, I'm inclined to believe that the boy may not fully meet the qualifications for Intersection 7."

"He is a traitor!"

Lance shifts his eyes away and murmurs, "A traitor, indeed."

"What do you want me to do?" I ask with a low, intense whisper.

Lance whispers back, "Be a beacon of hope. These people look up to you."

"They fear me."

"Would you rather be feared or respected?"

"Feared."

Lance's eyes narrow as he shakes his head. "Leading in this manner is not appropriate."

"I control."

"Paul, control isn't leadership."

There's a surge of power as I forcefully strike the podium, the sound reverberating. "Without fear and control, they'll tear me down. They'll dismantle everything I've built and worked for. At least the Implanted follow orders."

"They don't have a choice."

I find myself unable to contain my amusement. "It's interesting that you decide to voice your opinion now, when you've consistently supported my plans during our various briefings and discussions."

"I advocated for curbing aggression and criminality, to build a safer world for my children, not for turning people into mindless automatons and treating you as if you're almighty." Lance walks away. "This has spiraled out of control."

"Where are you going? You aren't dismissed, sir. Only your leader can dismiss you," I say, my voice heavy.

"Find a new judge," Lance says. "I'm done."

It's as though an invisible force is constricting my throat. My hands tremble, a sign of my faltering grip on the un-Implanted. That feeling creeps back up again; it's the fear putting me in a chokehold, sucking the breath from my lungs. I'm losing control. I march to the remaining Sons of Paul member and lean in close.

"Imprison him and his family."

"Yes, Mr. Randall," the soldier says. He follows his order and marches over to Lance. A wave of tension envelops me. I watch in silence as he handles Lance, forcibly throwing him to the ground and placing him under arrest. Lance's enraged outbursts and cursing only add to the moment's chaos.

"Paul, how could you!"

A sharp sting of tears forms at the edges of my eyes. It's a bitter realization to accept. Our friendship, nurtured in childhood innocence, once provided me with serenity. Still, now I am grappling to comprehend why he has chosen to oppose me, attacking me as though I am a despicable person. The painful truth is that I am losing my confidant.

I throw open the side door and step out of the room. As I make my way downstairs, the vehicle parked outside the glass doors comes into view, and I get in, just as tears begin streaming down my face. I use the back of my sleeve to quickly wipe them away. My mother's voice echoes in my mind. *Pull yourself together, Paul.* I sit up straighter.

Gathering my thoughts, I inhale deeply. I need to reassert control, and fast. When exactly did I lose my sway over the upper class? I wonder. How can I convince other leaders to allow Arkin to expand into their territory if I can't control my own people? I need to demonstrate that I can provide security. Within the next week or two, we have multiple contracts coming into effect, along with new implants currently being packaged to support this expansion.

The car's windows are fortified with bulletproof glass, and the car is crafted from the most durable and impenetrable material, albeit quite heavy. Every square inch of the vehicle is clean, from the floor mats free of any hints of dirt or lint to the aroma of leather that permeates the air. The scent of new leather is one of my favorite smells, with its clean and alluring essence; it reminds me of my childhood when my mother and I would visit my father's office for money. He possessed these big cushioned leather sofas and prohibited anyone from sitting on them. I remember wanting to sink into the cushions and drown myself in their comfort, but I didn't dare risk incurring my father's wrath. He'd strip the hide from my rear without considering who was around. He didn't care. So in those moments, I stood by my mother's side, leaning into her and relishing the warmth of her leg against my side, inhaling the rich scent of the leather.

"Where to, Mr. Randall?" Davis, the driver, asks, his gravelly voice breaking the silence in the car.

"Intersection 7," I say, rubbing my hands together.

The well-kept roads stretch before us, bordered by towering skyscrapers that sparkle in the sunlight. Numerous well-to-do families pause their activities and respectfully kneel as my vehicle passes them by. This tradition is a requirement and a display of deep respect.

"How is your day, Mr. Randall?"

"Everything's okay, Davis," I respond. "How's your day going? Are you having any issues with anyone?"

His eyes glance into the rearview mirror, looking back at me. "No trouble today, sir. None at all."

"Certainly. Certainly. Do you have everything you need? Is the vehicle in proper working condition? Is your family sufficiently provided for?"

"The car is spectacular. Much more secure than the last one," Davis says.

I lean in, my voice filled with determination. "I truly hope so. These rebels will go to any lengths to undermine our security. And your family? You didn't answer my question about them."

Davis hesitates. "They are doing very well."

"Has the baby been blessed?" I ask.

Davis glances into the mirror; the warmth of his expression is long gone. "Not yet, sir."

I nod. "He'll be blessed in the morning then."

"Well . . ."

"I will personally handle this matter." Davis appears hesitant, obviously wishing to express something. "Go on, Davis. Share your thoughts." *Everyone else is.*

"Mr. Randall, sir," Davis asks with a quivering voice, "what of the Implanted?"

"Thank you for raising this, Davis. The Implanted individuals have been preserved. The primary aim of their implantation is to ensure strict compliance with the specific regulations I have put in place."

"Are these regulations designed to provide security to the upper class? I've heard that the lower class is prone to violence and uncontrollable behavior, leading to the need for such security measures," Davis says. "I just heard . . . it was more for our safety."

I chuckle, holding back the urge to respond contemptuously to the notion that the Implanted and the rest of us are *safeguarded*. "Oh, certainly. This world is secure and free from danger but abundant with grace."

"What of the rebels? What will be done if the rebels breach?"

I take a deep breath. The heavy burden weighs on me as each day unfolds. I understand that his inquiries stem from his experiences as a new father. "Our sector is deemed the divine side. The rebels, well, I am committed to addressing this."

"Indeed, sir," Davis acknowledges, smoothly guiding the car to the side of the road and reducing its velocity. "Apologies for the questions."

"Questions are fine. Before I leave, Davis, I want to assure you there's no need to worry. You and your family are safe and secure," I say, smiling as I step out onto the curb.

The area is already filled with vehicles from the Sons of Paul, easily identifiable by their white color with the dove-and-vine emblem. Members of the Sons of Paul are patrolling the area, visibly armed. In the oppressive heat, citizens stand nearby, awaiting Nev's impending punishment. The air is thick with heat. Grass tinged with the faint aroma of gasoline. *Gasoline*. Strange . . .

As I make my way toward the front of the crowd to deliver my speech, several members of the Sons of Paul hurry over to escort me, ensuring my protection and security. We walk together in perfect unison, and the citizens respectfully kneel as I pass. It is a powerful display of unity. Preparations are being made to raise Nev high above the crowd. It's a disturbing spectacle reminiscent of the public executions of the fifteenth century.

I'm met with an overwhelming sea of expectant faces, their eyes fixed on me with hope and apprehension. The Sons of Paul implemented a new security measure in the form of a formidable panel of bulletproof glass, a stark reminder of the recent brutal acts of the rebels. I adjust the microphone to the perfect height, striving to maintain composure despite my shaking hands and the lump in my throat. The unnerving thought of a potential attack by the audience lingers in my mind, adding to the weight of responsibility on my shoulders.

"Move up just a bit, will you?"

The soldier abides.

Nev is standing underneath the tallest lamppost in the city, George by his side. His hands are bound in front of him, yet he holds his head high, showing no signs of fear. His parents are composed, just like George. I run my hands down the smooth, perfectly pressed fabric of my gray suit and take in a deep breath to calm my nerves.

"Ladies and gentlemen, good afternoon. We are here today to witness Nev Hurter's final moments. Nev, a dedicated and sworn-in member of the Sons of Paul, held a position of great trust within his unit and among his superiors. As the leader, or vine, of Arkin, the Sons of Paul are extensions, or branches, of my authority. I must take action against Mr. Hurter and ensure that he faces the consequences of his actions. Allowing him to go unpunished would set a dangerous precedent. Mr. Hurter's misconduct may contaminate other members or rot the remainder of the branches, leading to widespread corruption within our ranks. As the leader, it is my responsibility to safeguard the honor and unity of our organization, and I cannot tolerate any rotten branches that threaten the well-being of our people and mission."

I continue, "Regrettably, he abused this trust by accessing and sharing sensitive information that poses a significant threat to Arkin and its citizens: you and the Implanted. His actions occurred amid the rebellion, escalating tensions and leaving us running. Arkin is apprehensive about the rebels' next move. Their intentions with the information he provided are unknown. Therefore, the sentence has been passed. Nev stands condemned to death for his treacherous acts."

George places a metal hook around Nev's wrists at the center. The mechanism is a strange yet sturdy contraption designed of metal and rope, and I've witnessed this action a dozen times at this intersection. The extended cable, barely visible from down here, is assembled over the light post. Nev is secure. George keeps his head down. The arrogant youth is now reduced to my puppet in his friend's undoing.

Today is indeed a day of lost friendships.

George moves to the opposite side of the light post and grabs the cable, with several other members of the Sons of Paul following. Together, they grab hold of the cable and pull. With each tug, Nev's hands rise higher and higher until his arms are fully over his head and his feet lift off the ground. Nev grits his teeth and struggles to keep his eyes open, battling through waves of pain.

The birds caw loudly, sensing an imminent meal. The grueling effort persists until Nev is just ten feet above the ground, and I can almost make out the beads of sweat forming on his forehead. He's not even a third of the way up, and his shoulders already look like they're under severe pressure, ready to dislocate at any time now under his weight.

Suddenly, a member of the Sons of Paul collapses, sending a ripple of confusion through the crowd. Nev lowers closer to the ground as another member falls. The sound of gunfire echoes as more Sons of Paul are taken down, one by one. In an instant, bullets are pounding against the bulletproof panel in front of me, which provides only a temporary shield of safety. Panic ensues as people scatter in all directions. Amid the disorder, a wave of nausea sweeps over me, and I find myself vomiting onto my shoes.

I survey the area, and chaos erupts all around me. People screaming and running in every direction. I look to where Nev stood, but he is gone. George appears in front of me, so close that I can reach out and touch him.

"George, you're a good boy. Escort me to the car. You will leave with me," I say as I step out from behind the protective bulletproof glass and toward him.

That's when a significant explosion, followed by another, throws me to the ground. My face scuffs along the asphalt, and my skin peels off. It burns and is wet and sticky with blood. I push myself upright. My ears are ringing, and an iron tang fills my mouth. Panic sets in. I need to get to the car. I turn, and the vehicle is in cinders. I glance back to George, who's splayed on the ground. *Dead.* I rise as the remaining Sons of Paul members exchange fire with the cadre of hidden rebels.

A knot twists in my stomach as I sprint as fast as my aching body will allow. Every muscle in my legs protests, and a terrified scream escapes my lips as I make a beeline for the closest safe house. Several safe houses are placed all over the city if such situations arise. The issue is that I rely on a car to get me there in all my escape plans, and I now regret that.

After several minutes of sprinting, I am away from the gunfire and can finally slow down and catch my breath. Now that the chaos is subsiding, I can't help but feel a mix of emotions. I wonder how many of my Sons of Paul soldiers didn't make it through. It's a harsh reality, but I must focus on recruiting and building our numbers again.

I turn the corner and find myself face-to-face with the barrel of a gun. Intense green eyes stare at me over the weapon, and the glint of a metal eyebrow piercing catches my eye.

I'll never forget that face. It's engraved in my memory— *Irina.*

"You have some nerve, Paul."

I recoil, taking a step back. "I'm only trying to create a better world."

Her laughter rings out, sinister and suspicious. "Is it your vision of a utopia to hang people up and confine them within their bodies?"

"Well, yes," I say.

"A utopia *for who?*" She screams the question and pushes the barrel into my chest.

"Don't kill me," I plead. "Please."

"I'll kill you, but not today."

"How about we strike a deal, and no one dies."

"That's not how this will work. You will help me," she says.

I laugh. "What could I possibly help you with?"

"Freeing the Implanted."

I burst into laughter. "You're ridiculous, my dear. I will never assist you."

There's an intense jab against my back.

"You'll help her," the deep voice says.

Nev.

"Nev . . . you're alive."

"Save it, you coward," Nev hisses. "You're coming with us."

"I'll do no such thing."

Irina locks eyes with me, her gaze piercing. "Your document, Eden Falling, holds part of the key to freeing them. You're going to help me."

"I'd rather die."

"Oh really?" she says, removing the barrel from my chest and pointing it to the ground, pulling the trigger.

The scorching pain through my foot is excruciating and I collapse. "You little bitch!" My voice is almost hoarse. The fear rushing through my veins feels like a raging river, threatening to overwhelm me. But my desire for control burns even stronger than my fear. I refuse to let go of my grasp on this world. "You'll have to kill me first!"

"Well, that settles it." Irina moves the barrel of the gun to my forehead, her expression unreadable.

"Wait, wait," I say, raising my hands. "Let's have a conversation about this."

"I'm exhausted from indulging in your games and conversations. You've caused my family so much pain, and you almost killed Nev," Irina says, exhaustion evident in her voice as she crouches down to my eye level. You will instruct me and my team on removing the implant, or you will face the consequences. Do you understand?"

I try to calm my nerves so that I don't start crying. *Pull yourself together, Paul.* I can hear my mother's voice as if she were beside me.

"Okay," I mumble. Nev grabs me by the collar and lifts me to my feet. The pain shoots through my foot again. "I don't think I can walk."

Irina's cold voice cuts through the air. "You better learn how," she says without empathy. "After you."

As I take a step forward, my balance falters, and the throbbing pain intensifies. "Please," I whisper, pleading for relief.

"Go," Irina orders.

As I start walking, my mind becomes consumed by the teachings my mother passed on to me about forgiveness and navigating treacherous paths. She also taught me how to survive encounters with brutal individuals like Irina, and my father. I make a concerted effort to push aside the fear coursing through my veins—it's as palpable as the unbearable pain in my foot.

I have power and control. This is not the end, I mentally repeat, trying to hold onto a sense of agency and resilience.

With these thoughts at the forefront of my mind, I follow Irina. It may feel like the end, but I refuse to believe it is over.

NO ONE WILL DIE TODAY

DR. ELSHER

No one will die today."

At least, that's what Dr. Elsher tells herself as she stands in front of the bathroom sink, gripping the smooth porcelain. She tries to convince herself that today will be different. That's a hard sell, considering The Shield's recent attempts to liberate the Implanted from Paul Randall's control. But after multiple failed attempts, the removals have ceased.

Until today.

Dr. Elsher's unwavering commitment to preserving life is rooted in her childhood fascination with the beauty and resilience of living beings. She didn't know if she could witness another failed removal, not after watching multiple Implanted individuals perish at her hands. The image of them slinking to the floor haunts her. A sharp *thud* and the haunting vacancy in their eyes in those final moments.

She didn't want to think about all the blood. The newer implants differ from Kinley's first-generation, so what they know is futile. However, after losing Chey, they'd implemented a new protocol that everyone within five feet must wear a mask to shield themselves from the mist. At least their efforts hadn't been totally in vain.

The document Eden Falling, which Nev smuggled to the team, appeared promising. But they soon realized that vital sections were missing, and they'd have to track down Paul Randall to unravel the hidden secret—something that went far beyond what was initially apparent.

Irina had ordered Dr. Elsher to remain in the warehouse with Evander, Kinley, and three Implanted while she set out to rescue Nev and bring Paul Randall in. Failure is not an option, for any of them. When Irina reaches a decision, she pursues it with unwavering commitment, which is why Rebecca Gwynne, leader of The Shield, trusts her. Irina is certainly relentless.

Three sharp raps echo from the door behind her, snapping her out of her thoughts. Startled, she straightens up, running her hands down the length of her trousers.

"Yes?" she calls out, her voice tinged with uncertainty.

"Are you okay, Dr. Elsher?"

"Yes, Kinley. I'm fine."

"Are you sure?"

"Not really."

"It'll work this time. It has to," Kinley says.

With a gentle tug, the heavy door swings inward. Sunlight streams in through the doorway and catches Kinley's eyes, causing them to sparkle with a sense of liberation. The girl's radiant hay-colored hair glows in the light as she studies Dr. Elsher. Over time, Dr. Elsher has come to see Kinley as a younger sister. Evander, too, has been a positive presence in her life, proving to be a person many gravitate toward due to his understanding, kindness, and care. He and Kinley had grown very close, often spending their time with his small crew, which included Brooks, Jett, and Madison.

Dr. Elsher sighs. "I hope that's the case."

Kinley's gaze drifts away, her eyes scanning the weathered surface of the concrete pad as if searching for something elusive. The lines and cracks hold a story of their own.

"Remember, even though The Shield didn't have written documents or procedures at the time, it worked for me," Kinley says, forcing a smile. "I believe it will work for others, too. We have more knowledge now."

"That's a good point, Kin."

She smiles. "Plus, if Irina finds Paul Randall . . . that'll change everything . . ."

A loud, ominous bang reverberates as someone pounds on the main door. In a panic, she clutches Kinley's shoulder, her heart racing in her chest, as they both take cover behind a towering stack of musty boxes. Meanwhile, Evander maneuvers across the room into his secluded hiding spot where he can peek over the haphazardly piled boxes and keep a vigilant watch on the door. Dr. Elsher hopes the person outside is Irina and everything has gone according to plan. Though she puts on a brave front, Dr. Elsher remains gripped by fear of falling into the hands of the Sons of Paul.

A few minutes later, the heavy door bursts open with a resounding crash. A tall, lean figure stumbles into the dimly lit warehouse. His labored breathing fills the quiet space as he struggles to maintain his balance. His features are marked by distress rather than menace, and without uttering a single word, he presses onward, each step a noticeable effort, his determination etched in every strained movement.

As the man turns to face the door, Irina sweeps into the room with a commanding presence, her every movement exuding confidence. Nev follows closely behind, closing and securing the door. Nev's haggard physical appearance is evident in his sunken cheeks and the tired look in his eyes. Recent events have substantially impacted him, leaving him visibly fatigued.

"Everyone, this is Paul," Irina says.

With all eyes fixed on Paul, a hush falls over the room as everyone seems to freeze in place. Paul keeps his head lowered, avoiding all eye contact. This behavior is a stark departure from the usual assertiveness typically reserved for his intercom and television announcements. Paul now resembles a turtle retreating into its protective shell, the air of aggression and authority that characterized him as the leader of Arkin all but drained from him. He looks so ordinary and vulnerable.

Dr. Elsher extends a supportive hand and helps Kinley to her feet. Kinley looks at the man who had held her in a zombie-like state for so long, a mix of anger and concern evident on his face.

Evander smiles, his dimples appearing as he addresses her. "Dr. Elsher, I will stay with Kinley if you need to begin."

Dr. Elsher redirects her attention to Paul Randall, taking in his disheveled appearance. His clothes are caked with a fine layer of dust, and various stains mark the fabric. A deep, jagged cut mars the skin above his left eyebrow. His hair is a tangled mess, also coated in dust. The dim lighting in the warehouse casts a murky haze caused by layers of grime that coat the windows, giving the space an almost ethereal quality. Among the scattered pieces of machinery, the air hums with the faint sound of distant whirring and clanking. Towering piles of boxes dominate the space, their weathered exteriors telling stories of countless journeys and shipments.

As she approaches him, Paul Randall loses more of his usual healthy color, turning eerily pale. Dr. Elsher, with her experienced eye, detects a slight trembling in his hands. There's also a conspicuous and fresh wound on his foot.

Dr. Elsher swallows. "Irina, he needs medical attention."

"He does. He can wait until after he decides to help."

Dr. Elsher disagrees. Despite Paul Randall's evident pain, the man maintains his stance, showing remarkable resilience. Suppressing her initial impulse to speak out, Dr. Elsher takes a deep breath and nods. Paul Randall is considered their adversary, after all.

"Very well. Let's get started then," Dr. Elsher says as she strides over to the first Implanted individual.

In her haste, Irina firmly propels Paul into the operating area. It's far from ideal that Dr. Elsher has to use a warehouse for these procedures, but there's too much at stake and they're running out of options.

She removes the rough burlap sack from the Implanted's head. A shock of vibrant orange hair cascades over his eyes. Only in his midtwenties, the man appears remarkably young and incredibly vulnerable in light of the impending procedure. Evander steps forward while Kinley hangs back, her arms crossed as she witnesses the familiar spectacle. Dr. Elsher activates her handheld light and meticulously examines behind the man's ear for the telltale sign of a faint white scar. With precision, she continues her thorough search.

"It's in the forearm," she finally informs the group. "Evander, will you escort him to the operating chair?"

"Absolutely, Dr. Elsher," Evander responds with his trademark helpfulness. His pleasant and kind demeanor counterbalances Irina's direct and commanding approach. Despite Irina's strong personality, it's clear she means well and is passionate about restoring normalcy to the world.

"This," Dr. Elsher remarks, her finger tracing a comprehensive list of procedures in a document before her, "is the pivotal moment where everything begins to unravel." She gazes intently at Paul Randall as the Implanted is fastened to the operating chair.

Irina, with a determined look, leads Paul Randall to Dr. Elsher, almost pushing him. "Share with her all the information that she needs to know."

Paul staggers forward, legs trembling, hands unable to stay still. His lips tense into a tight line as he says, "I won't help you until I receive proper treatment. Besides, you already released her. You must know what you're doing." He nods at Kinley and flashes a sinister smile.

Kinley quietly steps directly behind Evander, whose hands tighten into fists at his sides, his knuckles turning white as his emotions swell.

"I understand this must be an incredibly challenging situation for you. The prospect of seeing something you worked hard to create and passionately believe in being altered, deactivated, or even taken away is truly difficult to fathom," Dr. Elsher says with empathy and understanding. "Nonetheless, Paul, it's important to consider that these individuals deserve the chance to truly live and fully experience life, rather than merely existing."

With a lingering glance in Kinley's direction, Paul murmurs, "She was the first. An unfortunate implant. Flawed and far too simple to bypass." Paul's gaze locks onto Dr. Elsher, his hands once trembling with emotion now unnervingly still as he adds, "My foot."

Dr. Elsher, feeling the strain in her eyes, wearily rubs them with the back of her hand. "Irina, please let me give him some pain medicine and apply a wrap to provide some relief at the very least."

Irina lets out a heavy sigh before finally giving in. "Very well, go ahead and patch him up."

"Get him a chair," Dr. Elsher says.

Dr. Elsher washes her hands with antibacterial soap, then gathers the necessary supplies: pain medicine, antiseptic solution, sterile white gauze, and a soft wrap to shield and support the wound. With deliberate and cautious movements, she hands Paul the medicine and carefully kneels in front of him, gently cradling his foot. She places it on her knee to begin the meticulous process of cleansing and dressing the wound.

"Please, allow me," Evander offers as he carefully removes Paul Randall's shoe and damp sock.

The injury is quite severe. A deep hole runs from the top of the foot to the sole. It will likely take a considerable amount of time to heal, with no guarantee it will ever fully heal. He may have a permanent limp.

As Dr. Elsher cleans the wound to prevent infection and wraps his injured foot, Paul Randall's gaze remains fixed on her, displaying gratitude and apprehension.

Dr. Elsher leans forward in her chair. Her voice is confident and compelling. "So, are you ready to assist me, Paul?"

He chuckles and shakes his head. "I won't assist you."

Dr. Elsher hesitates momentarily, taking a deep breath as she contemplates her next move. After a brief pause, she decides to revise her approach. "What if I proposed that we attempt to reach a mutually beneficial agreement?"

"There's no deal with you insurgents. You'll have me killed."

"What if I guaranteed your safety? Your life in exchange for helping me?"

Irina's eyes widen in astonishment, her breath catching at the unexpected suggestion.

After considering her words, Paul furrows his brow and with a subtle note of doubt responds, "I have to confess, I'm finding it rather difficult to place my trust in you fully."

"Can the rest of you excuse us?" Dr. Elsher asks the group.

"I can't leave you alone with him," Irina says.

"Keep his hands bound. Do any necessary physical actions, but I want to speak with him, alone."

Paul remains impassive, showing little to no emotion. Irina glances from Nev to Evander, then to Kinley, Paul, and finally back to Dr. Elsher. After a brief pause, she nods and instructs Evander. "Secure his legs. Connect a chain from the restraints on his hands to the ones around his ankles."

The links of the heavy iron chains show signs of wear and tear from the passage of time and repeated use. With meticulous precision, Evander fastens the chains from Paul's wrists to his ankles, the metallic *clinks* echoing through the vast expanse of the warehouse, punctuating the oppressive silence.

Once the chains are secure, the group sets off to the distant corner of the warehouse, allowing her to have the necessary space to concentrate on her work without any distractions. Performing procedures with extra eyes around always makes her uneasy.

Dr. Elsher remains in the operating area, the sterile scent of disinfectant hanging in the air. Her palms glisten with nervous sweat, and she absentmindedly intertwines her fingers, a childhood habit that often resurfaces during moments of anxiety. As a skilled surgeon, she relies on the tactile comfort of her hands when examining or calming nervous patients and finds solace in the reassuring touch.

"Let's try this again, Paul. I've been diligently working on extracting these implants," she says, her voice steady despite the undercurrent of tension in the room. "Everything has been progressing smoothly until . . ." She pauses, flipping through Eden Falling until she finds the section she's looking for. "Right here," she points out. "There's a critical detail that your team overlooked and failed to include in this document."

Paul seems completely disinterested in the document between them. He shifts in his seat, adjusting his posture, and takes a long, deliberate breath. "That was intentional," he says, breaking the silence that had settled over them.

Dr. Elsher gives him the needed time, observing his hands tremble again. She can't help but empathize with him a little, recognizing their shared experience of nervous fidgeting. This moment is a powerful reminder of their common humanity, transcending their apparent differences.

"Are you feeling apprehensive?" Without pausing for a response, she adds, "I can relate to that sentiment all too well. As a child, I grappled with anxiety and didn't have a supportive parent to turn to for comfort and understanding. I had to discover ways to channel that anxiety away from consuming me, slowly but surely." She detects a slight shift in his demeanor. "When you lack someone to share your feelings with, or worse, face punishment for expressing them, it profoundly changes you. It shapes your outlook on life and others, often fostering a sense of doubt. That's why I pursued a medical career—to help individuals at their most vulnerable confront their fears. When they confront the stark reality of their illness or fear for their lives, I'm there for them because I didn't have that support when I needed it the most."

Paul fidgets in his seat.

Dr. Elsher continues, sensing she's getting somewhere. "These people—the Implanted—are gripped by fear, Paul, and you wouldn't want that for anyone."

"The implants are *saving* them."

"In what way?"

"Their souls cannot be stained by corruption. The implants act as a barrier, protecting their essence from any form of moral or spiritual decay."

"Paul . . ."

"They feel no fear. I've cured them. I've saved them."

Dr. Elsher's furrowed brow harbors a deep concern. "You are *controlling* them," she says. A subtle flash in his eyes prompts her to step back instinctively. "Yes, I understand it's in their best interest. But what if they have learned from your implant? What if they have changed and can make better choices because of it?"

"Enough!" he declares, raising his head. "If I choose to assist you, what will happen to me afterward?"

"You live."

He laughs. "Your friend Irina wouldn't dare let that happen."

Dr. Elsher locks eyes with him. "Irina will have to consent to our decision, if you decide to offer your assistance."

"How can you assure that?" he asks with skepticism.

"I have a close relationship with The Shield's leader."

"Is that what you call yourselves?"

"It's no worse than the Sons of Paul," she retorts.

His lips curl upward, forming a genuine smile that reaches his suddenly warm, expressive eyes. "Dr. Elsher, is it?" he asks.

She nods. "Yes, that's right."

"We connect as if we intuitively grasp each other's thoughts and feelings. I'll assist you."

Dr. Elsher's heart races in her chest with relief at the positive response. "Do you really mean it?"

"Ensure my safety," he says.

"I will."

"Say it."

"Say what?"

"That you, Dr. Elsher, will guarantee my safety with your life," he demands, his eyes unwavering.

"I, Dr. Elsher, will guarantee your safety with my life," she says.

"Good. Let's get started."

Dr. Elsher's lips quiver with restrained amusement as she fights back a smile. "Just give me a moment to discuss with my group" she says, gesturing Irina and the others over.

"He'll help," she tells them.

Irina's gaze bores into her. She's clearly suspicious. "You made a deal with him."

Dr. Elsher meets her gaze. "I did."

"What was it?"

"What I said it'd be. He helps us, and we spare his life." Dr. Elsher holds her ground even though she knows they won't agree with her.

Irina's eyes widen in disbelief, her mouth gaping open in shock. Nev stands frozen; his usually composed demeanor shatters in an instant. He appears as though he's been struck down by an invisible force, leaving him breathless and speechless. Evander and Kinley exchange a brief glance; their downcast eyes betray their disapproval and their subtle gestures communicate volumes without a single word being spoken.

"We can't allow deals. Not like this," Irina says on behalf of the group.

"You have to," Dr. Elsher says.

"After we've gathered all the essential information, we'll no longer be reliant on his guidance," Nev says, his once glowing complexion now dimmed by the streaks of dirt that adorn his face.

Dr. Elsher raises her hands. "Listen, we may need him. The full range of potential variations in implants remains unknown to us. Keeping him alive is a precautionary measure that could prove crucial in addressing potential complications."

Irina, visibly frustrated, releases a weary sigh. After a moment, she finally relents. "Fine."

Dr. Elsher's lips curve into a barely noticeable smile as she addresses the group. "To reiterate, Paul Randall assists us, and in return we commit to ensuring his safety. Are we all in consensus regarding this?"

"We are in consensus," Irina says. "We'll let you work. Let us know if you need anything."

"Great. Retrieve the red-haired one and position a mask over his nose and mouth." She looks over the group. "You all wear one, too. Most forearm implants don't have the mist, but as I said, I don't know how many variations are out there."

She returns to Paul, who's sitting motionless, seemingly lost in a whirlwind of contemplation while the world swirls around him.

"Dr. Elsher?" Kinley has stayed back, something clearly on her mind.

"I'm finding it difficult to articulate this." Her words are tinged with uncertainty.

Dr. Elsher responds with a warm smile. "Please, feel comfortable expressing yourself openly."

Kinley fixes her gaze on Paul Randall, her expression a mix of caution and worry. "I wouldn't trust him. He's . . . cunning."

Dr. Elsher tilts her head to the side, her eyes shimmering with curiosity. "I'd imagine he'd have to be quite charismatic to have gathered such a devoted following. What's troubling you, Kin?"

Kinley shifts on her feet, her eyes flitting back and forth as she speaks. "He . . . just can't be trusted. When all this happened, I saw things . . . he knows how to manipulate and maneuver."

Dr. Elsher places a reassuring hand on Kinley's shoulder. "It's going to be okay. I believe I've made some headway with him. There's no indication that he would take any actions to endanger his own life."

Kinley sighs. "You don't understand."

"Kinley," Dr. Elsher says, "I understand that you may have seen something distressing, but I want to reassure you that Paul Randall is just an ordinary man. Here, you are safe, and there's no need to worry."

"I'm asking you to please be cautious," Kinley says, averting her eyes.

"Absolutely," Dr. Elsher responds.

* * *

Dr. Elsher inspects and sanitizes each surgical instrument, ensuring nothing is overlooked as she prepares for the surgery. She maintains a calm and focused demeanor that exudes a palpable sense of determination and anticipation for the task ahead.

This had to work.

"Paul, I can assure you that your safety is our top priority."

"That's reassuring to hear."

"I've given you my assurance," Dr. Elsher reiterates.

"Let's hope you follow through on that promise."

With profound responsibility and care, Dr. Elsher begins by placing a sterile mask over the Implanted and Paul, ensuring a snug fit for maximum protection, then carefully positions a small bright light over the precise operating area.

She takes a moment to cleanse her hands, then pulls on sterile gloves.

"Paul, are you ready?"

Paul's eyes take on a steely intensity. "Go on."

"Could you please confirm that everything from the point I mentioned earlier is accurate?"

"It is."

"Perfect. So, I'll get started, and once I'm at that point, you'll walk me through it, correct?"

"That's what we agreed on."

As Dr. Elsher prepares to perform the intricate procedure, she carefully administers a local anesthetic to the patient's forearm. With a steady hand, she creates a small incision with her scalpel, revealing the silver implant beneath the tender tissue.

She navigates the complex web of tissue surrounding the implant, making sure to preserve the intricate network that extends into the patient's body. With her exceptional expertise, she manages to extract the tissue while safeguarding the implant's complicated structure, which was originally designed to integrate and become embedded within the individual for maximum control.

"It's time, Paul."

He averts his gaze momentarily and then shifts his attention back to her. "The smaller branches . . ."

"Branches? The tentacles?"

"The implant has branches that resemble extensions from a vine. These branches can be cut without any problems, so let's begin there. There are eight small branches, with two located at each corner. Cut each of these branches. They will bleed significantly, but the bleeding should stop after approximately twenty seconds," Paul says.

She squints, carefully examining the delicate offshoots—not tentacles—that extend from each corner, twisting in intricate patterns. There are two larger appendages at the outer edges of the implant, resembling thick, bluish-purple veins. She decides to forgo inspecting those for the time being and proceeds to cut off the first minuscule branch. As she snips it, a crimson fluid begins to well up. She allows twenty seconds to pass before wiping away the liquid.

Dr. Elsher continues the surgical process, severing the smaller branches of the affected area one by one and cleansing each before moving on to the next. As the final branch is cut, Dr. Elsher exhales and allows herself a small, satisfied smile, even though it's hidden behind her surgical mask. There is no sign of any fatal complications; the patient did not even suffer excessive bleeding. The procedure has been a success so far.

Dr. Elsher looks at Paul. "What next?"

"The larger bottom branch displays a beautiful transition from deep purple at the base to a vibrant blue at the top. Do you see it?"

"I see it."

"Cut just above where the color transitions. Make sure it's not too high or too low; aim for a smooth transition between the colors," Paul says.

She takes a deep breath and decides on the perfect spot in the transition to cut. The branches here are a little more sturdy to cut through, but she does it, nonetheless. Blood pools up, and she cleans the wound again. The procedure is nearing completion, and the implant is almost detached. She's confident in Paul Randall's integrity once an agreement is reached. He isn't evil; he's like a man with an apprehensive child hidden beneath the exterior.

With a satisfied smile, she gazes up from her work. "Finished."

"Pull the bottom half of the severed branch out," Paul instructs.

Dr. Elsher switches instruments, exchanging the worn-out tool for a sturdier one. With a firm grip, she seizes the lower half of the stubborn branch and applies a powerful, sustained pressure. After several intense tugs, it finally breaks free, leaving Dr. Elsher with the realization that the Implanted will feel the pain of her exertions tomorrow.

"Paul?"

Paul locks eyes with her, his gaze holding an unusual intensity. His eyes appear different, less bright and clear, almost as if a shadow has passed over them. "Dr. Elsher," he murmurs.

"What next?"

"What'd you do to the other branches?"

"I severed them and did a little pulling."

"Go on then."

She hesitates, uncertain about following his limited direction, which startles her. "I've severed it before on other occasions, and they either bled out or there was a fatal mist."

"True. Do you remember where you cut?"

"Yes."

"Well, cut in between those areas."

"That's it?"

He nods—his focus intent on the work at hand.

She picks up the scalpel, places it where she knows the spot is, and clips it. The Implanted starts bleeding profusely. Dr. Elsher tries to save him, to stop it.

"Paul . . ."

Dr. Elsher panics as she struggles to stop the bleeding. The Implanted slumps in the chair, their body sliding and thudding over the side. Dr. Elsher's eyes well up with tears, her chest heaving as she struggles to catch her breath. This is exactly how it happened the other times. *Thud*, vacant stares.

The weight of Paul Randall's despicable and truly evil actions is overwhelming. Faced with such deep betrayal, Dr. Elsher wrestles with how she can honor her end of the deal.

As she presses her palms flat against the cool, smooth surface of the table, she takes a steadying breath. His extensive knowledge holds the crucial information they need to remove the implants, and without his cooperation, they'll have no choice but to persist with their risky experiments. More people will die.

Dr. Elsher's attention is caught by the faint sound of feet against the worn concrete. Irina freezes in her tracks, her gaze fixed on the figure of the red-headed Implanted, head lolling to the side.

"What happened?" Irina asks, looking between Paul and Dr. Elsher. Her eyes narrow. Paul responds by lifting his chin slightly and peering down at her with an inscrutable expression, his eyes giving nothing away.

"I made the incision too high," Dr. Elsher says, straightening up.

"He didn't tell you otherwise?" Irina asks.

Dr. Elsher says, "The situation is quite complex."

Paul glances at her, his expression pensive as he absorbs her words.

Irina hesitates as she weighs the decision. Finally, she lets out a small sigh and shrugs. "Alright, I guess."

As Irina removes the Implanted from the chair, dragging him away, Dr. Elsher begins cleaning and sanitizing the operating chair for their next attempt.

When they're alone again, Paul whispers to Dr. Elsher, "Is my life still guaranteed?"

Dr. Elsher shifts on her heel, her eyes flashing with suppressed anger as she holds back the seething words on the tip of her tongue. "Yes. I keep my promises, but you need to understand that if you do that again, I won't be able to support you any longer." Dr. Elsher's voice is barely audible as she struggles to maintain her composure. "The trust I've established and the care I offer to these individuals mean a great deal to me, and your actions have jeopardized that trust. I'm working to save them, just as you do, albeit in a different way. We may have similarities in our methods, but we are also different. If this happens again, it will show that we are more distinct than I had ever realized."

He sighs. "But we are vastly different, Dr. Elsher. Had you acted as I just did, you'd be dead by now."

Dr. Elsher narrows her eyes. "Do you acknowledge you should be responsible for your actions?"

"Absolutely not. I'm only pointing out that you covered for me, and I wouldn't have done the same," Paul Randall says, looking away from her.

He would have killed her.

"Are you worried about losing your standing?" she asks, the question heavy on her mind.

"I constantly struggle with the fear of losing control. The thought of facing mortality is daunting, which is why I'm willing to work together and find a resolution. I apologize for . . . that."

"For what?"

"What I did. Misdirecting you. I like to test people to extremes, for them to prove their loyalty to me."

Dr. Elsher gives a subtle nod of acknowledgment as Irina approaches with the next Implanted. She guides him into the seat with a gentle touch, showing great tenderness and consideration.

"Dr. Elsher, may I have a moment?" Irina asks, leading her to a more private location out of earshot.

"What's going on?"

"That Implanted . . . it's my brother," Irina pleads. "I can't watch if he were to die. Still, he deserves a chance—to be free. If not . . . well, at least he will help us move forward."

Dr. Elsher offers her a reassuring squeeze. "Don't worry, he's going to be just fine. Just . . . stay out of eyesight . . . just in case. I'll begin right away."

Irina's typically strong and resolute demeanor melts away to reveal a rare vulnerability as she nods. Dr. Elsher can't help but notice the fragility, worry, and concern etched on Irina's face—a side of her that she hasn't witnessed before. Dr. Elsher secretly feels grateful to Irina for pulling her away from Paul to deliver the news. If Irina hadn't, the same unfortunate situation would likely have repeated itself once more.

Despite the vacant look in the patient's eyes, Dr. Elsher discerns a youthful and striking handsomeness. His dark hair and piercing green eyes are much like his sister's.

She scans for the faint scar and eventually locates it on his forearm.

"Should I proceed as last time?"

Paul nods. "Until the last branch."

Dr. Elsher works with precision, severing each branch and soaking up the pools of blood that bubble up. When she gets to the last branch, the big one, she looks to Paul for instruction.

Paul takes a deep breath before explaining the process in detail. "First, firmly grip the branch at its base using these tools," he gestures to the tray, "and then you'll need to exert a downward pull while simultaneously pushing the implant inward, slowly and steadily."

"Cutting?"

"Cutting will kill him."

"Okay," Dr. Elsher says. "Like this?"

"Slower. Be careful."

She applies gentle pressure to the branch, using a specialized tool to put pressure on the implant. She receives a reassuring nod from Paul as she painstakingly withdraws the slender branch, which seems to extend endlessly. Finally, as she nears the end, she discovers that it's firmly connected to a delicate vein.

"Those white spiderweb things growing from it . . . burn them."

She carefully selects the tool for treating minor burns and burns away the webbing.

As she stands in the sterile operating area, the bright lights glinting off the steel surfaces, she hears a sudden sharp gasp. The Implanted's chest is rising and falling with rapid breaths, free from its robotic paralysis, and as she properly meets the piercing green eyes for the first time, elation washes over her.

"Don't move," she instructs, her voice calm but her eyes betraying a hint of excitement as she stitches up the wound.

The Implanted smiles and tears emerge simultaneously. "I'm Heath . . . my sister . . ."

"Irina."

"We need to find her," Heath says, remaining as still as possible to listen for any signs of her.

"She's here."

"Earlier, I thought I heard her voice, but I wasn't completely sure," he says, a bright smile breaking through the tears.

"I'll bring you to her," she says. Her gaze turns to Paul. "Anything else?"

"No. That's it," Paul says.

"Thank you, Paul."

He turns away, his head sinking under the heavy burden of defeat that surrounds him.

Heath expresses a sense of total awareness and a lack of control, describing it as the worst feeling. He then asks, "How many others have you liberated?"

"Only one. Her name is Kinley. She's here," Dr. Elsher says.

"Two? We're it?" There's a lot of work ahead of us then."

Dr. Elsher smiles. "There is. You're all stitched up now. Let me take you to see your sister." She offers Heath a supportive hand, helping him out of the chair.

"Sorry, I haven't had conscious control in a while. This feels strange," he says with a smile.

Dr. Elsher takes Heath around the bend where the rest of the group is seated on wooden crates and rusty chairs. As they enter, Irina's entire demeanor changes: the relentless rebel in her softens as she rushes toward Heath, wrapping her arms around him. Heath reciprocates with a warm smile as he embraces his sister. Dr. Elsher takes a step back, giving the siblings space to reconnect and share these heartfelt moments.

Afterward, as Dr. Elsher retraces her steps back to the procedure area, Irina falls into stride behind her, her gentle footsteps barely audible. She clears her throat and says, "Thank you." Her eyes sparkle with genuine gratitude and happiness.

"You're welcome."

"Dr. Elsher, prepare yourself for what lies ahead. We're on the verge of a new world, and I hope you're fully prepared for what's to come."

Dr. Elsher smiles. "Bring it on."

THE CODE OF HOPE

IRINA

Liberating Kinley and cracking the first-gen implant was a turning point for The Shield. This pivotal moment was followed by Dr. Elsher's persuasive efforts, leading to Paul Randall's decision to abandon the life he had whole-heartedly devoted himself to and instructing Irina's team on removing the implants. The repercussions of these series of wins for the rebels profoundly altered the trajectory of society, catalyzing a fundamental reshaping of society over the next three years.

The memory of seeing the profound alertness that filled Heath's eyes once the implant was removed was etched deeply in Irina's mind. The overwhelming relief she experienced as he emerged from his zombie-like state was like a miraculous painting, the sense of accomplishment and joy as he returned to himself. The siblings' immediate priority was locating their mother, and this process was filled with moments of frustration, hope, and determination. It took weeks of relentless effort, but they eventually found her, and their reunion was profoundly emotional and heartfelt. The family's bond grew even stronger after overcoming the challenges posed by the implants, bringing them closer together in ways they had not thought possible.

Meanwhile, Dr. Elsher and her team worked to remove the individual implants. It was slow but steady progress, marked by small victories and hard-fought advancements in this arduous but hopeful journey toward reconstruction.

After many years, Irina had finally found a place she could call her own. Thanks to The Shield, she could select from various accommodations, each more luxurious than the last. She could have chosen a luxurious and expansive high-rise apartment. However, she'd decided on a modest two-bedroom apartment in a middle-class neighborhood on the East side. Despite its location, the apartment was in remarkable condition, a rare find in a city undergoing extensive change. The rest of the city had nearly fallen into advanced decay due to neglect and lack of maintenance.

"Come on, Eevee," Irina called out to her adorable tan and white French Bulldog puppy, who perked up and tilted her head from her spot on the cozy pink bed. "Coffee?"

Irina's gaze shifted to the unremarkable clock hanging on the worn wall. Its ticking was a constant reminder of the monumental task of rebuilding society after the cataclysm. Once readily available, items had to be painstakingly recreated through ingenuity and sheer determination. The most significant change, however, was the gradual restoration of normalcy, with resources becoming more abundant. Despite this progress, goods remained scarce, and Rebecca Gwynne and her dedicated team toiled tirelessly to reestablish order in the world.

Eevee waited for Irina to secure the purple harness around her, a daily routine that signaled the start of their day. Every morning, she would stroll to her favorite coffee shop and savor the simple joy of sipping a steaming cup of coffee while Eevee devoured whipped cream. Irina had never appreciated this routine until the day it was no longer possible. Supplies may have been low, but coffee beans were a necessity. The flavoring was … more challenging to obtain.

"Mom, I'm about to leave," Irina called out.

Her mother peered around the corner. "Have fun, dear. I'll be here when you get back. Do you want to watch a movie later?"

"Of course," Irina said, smiling. "I can pick up snacks."

"Sure, that sounds great. And if they happen to have any of those delicious little sour candies, could you pick some up for me, please?"

"You know it." Irina hoped they had a new batch of those colorful, tangy candies to appeal to her mother. She could be so childlike and vibrant these days.

On Fridays at five o'clock, Mom would come over and have a movie night. They would take turns picking movies and spend hours deciding on the perfect one. Once they settled on a movie, Mom, Heath, and Irina would relax on the cozy, overstuffed couch surrounded by snacks—popcorn, candy, and anything else that could be found at the store. They would chat and laugh, enjoying each other's company. It was a cherished ritual for them, a special time to bond and create lasting memories. Despite living in neighboring apartments in the same building, they treasured the closeness of their relationship while also valuing a bit of personal space.

As Irina and Eevee emerged from the building, the gentle caress of the sun's warmth enveloped them, casting a golden glow on everything it touched. On their way, they exchanged nods and warm smiles with the fellow pedestrians they encountered. Eevee took in the city's scents, detecting a delicate blend of fragrant flowers intermingled with the faint whiffs of gasoline from passing cars. One significant change was that now anyone could operate a vehicle. There were no longer any restrictions on who could drive. On the city's East side, anyway. The rest of the city was still home to the Implanted, who had not yet achieved complete freedom.

Irina was a symbol of hope to many, revered as a valiant crusader who had liberated countless individuals from the oppressive implants and the despotic reign of Paul Randall. Everywhere they went, people sought updates on Paul's whereabouts and ongoing activities. Despite her outward composure, Irina couldn't shake the sense of apprehension and resentment that gnawed at her. The possibility of Paul still exerting clandestine influence from his confines troubled her deeply. His remaining loyalists needed to be watched. And stopped.

A few times, his supporters came remarkably close to regaining control. However, the city's new leader and founder of The Shield, Rebecca Gwynne, strongly opposed Irina's unwavering determination for their complete eradication. Factions were forming.

Irina turned onto a quaint cobblestone street, which was lined with a handful of charming shops that had recently opened within the historic red-brick buildings, and stepped into the newly opened Espresso-self. The rich and delightful scent of freshly ground coffee beans filled the air, extending a warm welcome to everyone who entered. Eevee barked enthusiastically as she always did. The cozy space was adorned with abundant, vibrant plants. A large window at the front offered a picturesque view of the street, allowing visitors to take in the sights and sounds of the neighborhood.

"Eevee!" The group was all there—Evander, Madison, and the kids were seated across from Kinley, Nev, and Dr. Elsher, with the latest addition, Heath. They all stood up and clapped as the excitable pup jerked her leash from Irina's grasp, burning the palm of her hand. Irina's warm smile spread across her face as she greeted everyone. Her mind drifted back to the first time she'd encountered Evander and the kids—so frail, malnourished, and visibly terrified. She had brought them back here, to the once abandoned storefront, and now they were well-fed, had a sparkle in their eyes, and wore bright smiles as they played with Eevee. The transformation filled Irina's heart with joy and deep fulfillment.

The coffee shop was reminiscent of the original, which had been her Saturday morning sanctuary before the cataclysm, then later a refuge for newcomers to The Shield. New establishments were springing up, and it had recently been reopened. "The usual?" Jake, the owner, said from behind the counter.

"And the usual for the princess here." She pointed to Eevee, who sat in Kinley's lap lavishing all the attention.

Jake laughed. "You got it."

As he busied himself with preparing the order, Irina settled into the vacant seat at the far end of the table.

"When will Rebecca finally understand?" Nev said, his frustration boiling over. "We need to take action!"

Irina shifted in her seat, sitting upright. Nev's direct way of speaking indicated that something was not right. She was aware of the growing tensions within The Shield. "What's going on?" she said.

Jake placed her iced coffee in front of her and a cup of homemade whipped cream for Eevee, who lapped it up with evident delight, her vibrant green eyes closing in pure contentment. As she took her first sip, she couldn't help but smile at the sight of the children gathered around Eevee and Kinley. Their joyful laughter filled the air as they showered Eevee with affectionate pats and ear scratches. Despite the internal tensions brewing on how to deal with Paul's supporters, she felt a heartwarming and overwhelming sense of love and happiness for her friends.

Dr. Elsher cleared her throat, a look of concern on her face. "There are problems."

Irina looked around the group and said, "It's quite evident."

"Always be honest with her," advised Heath. "It's always better to be straightforward because if she detects any inconsistencies in your story, it could be the end for you." He winked.

"Be quiet, Heath," Irina said sternly, then turned to Nev, urging him to elaborate. "Nev, what's happened?"

"An attempt was made to liberate Paul Randall."

Heath reclined in his chair, an enigmatic smile tugging at the corners of his mouth as he savored a sip of his freshly brewed, aromatic coffee. "Don't stop now; go ahead and tell her what happened next," he encouraged.

"Rebecca's life was endangered in an attempted attack. She's receiving medical care in the hospital," said Dr. Elsher.

Evander tapped his fingers on the table, a troubled expression revealing the weight of the situation. "There were guards who were bribed to assist. Paul was on the brink of escaping, closer than anyone could have envisioned."

Irina's brows furrowed. "Dr. Elsher, I recall that both of you had come to an agreement. There was a clear understanding between you two, wasn't there?"

Dr. Elsher paused, looking unsure. "Yes, he was quite approachable initially. However, recently he's started to keep to himself more, and his behavior has become unpredictable."

Irina fought the urge to express her emotions and focused instead on sorting through the thoughts swirling in her mind. In the chaos, one thought stood out—her gaze landed on Eevee, the adorable puppy with a whipped cream mustache, and she couldn't help but break into a fond smile.

"I know that look. Her mind is running wild," Heath said.

Irina peeled her eyes from Eevee, feeling exasperated, rolled her eyes, and retorted, "Heath, shut up," drawing the attention of everyone at the table. She explained, "I'm okay; I have so many questions running through my mind right now."

"We all do," Kinley muttered.

"We must remember that he was stopped," Dr. Elsher said.

"That," Irina exclaimed, her eyes lighting up with determination, "is exactly what we should focus on. Let's direct our attention to the good things." Nev and Heath stared at her in surprise, their expressions changing from confusion to curiosity. "What?" she asked.

"That's unlike you," Heath said. "You're a pessimist."

Nev reached out and flicked Heath on the arm. With a stern look, he said, "Don't talk to her like that."

"She's my sister."

Nev's cheeks turned deep crimson and he looked down at his hands.

"I just can't bear worrying about Paul Randall for the rest of my life," Irina said.

The group nodded. They were all on the same page.

"Let's talk about something lighter. This makes my heart race," Kinley said.

They reminisced about life before the implants and found comfort in the progress that had been made over these last three years. Despite the lingering abnormality in Arkin, there was an overall feeling of improvement.

Irina, though thoroughly enjoying the conversation and the time spent with her friends, found herself preoccupied with thoughts of Paul Randall. His name kept intruding into her mind and she never felt fully present. Maybe she never would, with the constant threat of his escape. Glancing at the clock, she was surprised that forty-five minutes had flown by. As she toyed with leaving, she tentatively placed her hands on the table and said, "I think it's time for me to head out. Mom has been craving sour candies, and I'd like to pick some up for her."

Kinley embraced Eevee, holding her tight. "She doesn't want to leave."

"Yeah, she wants to stay with us," Madison, Brooks, and Jett said in unison.

"Would you mind bringing her to me around dinner-time? Take her on a walk, maybe even to the park. You know how she adores being around other animals and getting out of the apartment."

"Really?"

"Really," Irina said. "How about you all stop by tonight? It would be wonderful for Mom to have all of you over for a movie night."

The entire group accepted the invitation. They were excited about snacking on whatever treats Irina could find.

Irina pressed her lips against the top of Eevee's head—after all, Eevee was like a daughter. Leaving the cozy ambiance of the coffee shop behind, she set off on a walk toward the nearby shops known for their fresh snacks. However, as she drew closer to the sought-after shops, she veered right, deftly navigating through a maze of side streets until she arrived at her destination: headquarters.

* * *

The skyscraper was so clear it seemed to sparkle to the top, catching the sun's rays and reflecting them with a subtle blue glow. The crisp, refreshing air enveloped her as she entered the imposing main lobby. She made her way across polished black tile to the elevators; the guards all acknowledged her with a measured nod. Her identity was widely known, as no one dared to question her. She hastened to her locker on the third floor and retrieved the small object. Holding it in her hand, she took a deep breath and wondered if she was overreacting.

Deep down she knew this was what she needed to do.

She pocketed the object and took the elevator to the thirteenth floor. The rapid ascent caused her stomach to churn, and as she neared her destination, her anxiety only intensified.

She knew there would be only one guard stationed on the floor. As the elevator doors slid open, the guard's head snapped in her direction, his gaze following her every step as she approached him. He was clothed entirely in black, a stark contrast to the Sons of Paul's pristine white attire.

"I need the key to 1305," she said.

The guard hesitated. "I know who you are."

"Then that's all the more reason for you to hand me the key."

The guard averted his gaze, his well-defined jawline emphasized by his tanned skin. "You've placed me in a rather precarious situation."

"One day, we all may be in a precarious situation if Paul Randall is not subdued."

The guard nodded. "You have a five-minute window."

"Thank you."

"Irina," the guard said over his shoulder. "I never saw you. No one ever saw you—I'll ensure it."

"Got it."

"Be quick."

"The key?"

"Code. It's 0519."

The day we were liberated from Paul Randall. "That's easy to figure out."

"It's temporary after last night. Go."

She walked through the softly illuminated corridor, each step echoing faintly in the quiet space, until she came to door 1305. After inputting the code, the door clicked, and she pushed it open, stepping into the room.

Paul Randall was reclined on the neatly made bed in his modestly sized room. It smelled clean, almost like Clorox. While not expansive, the space provided all the necessities: a comfortable bed, a small couch, a private bathroom, and a television. These accommodations were provided as a token of appreciation for his assistance in removing the implants despite being their creator.

His gravelly voice cut through the air. "What do you want, girl?"

Irina gritted her teeth. "To see you."

His arrogant smile revealed the full extent of his conceit. "To see me."

His reaction told her everything she needed to know. "You're chipper."

Paul Randall remained seated on the bed, his long legs stretched before him. He looked relaxed in his neatly buttoned white shirt and dress pants, as if he had just returned home after a long day at work and was taking a well-deserved break.

His eyes cut to her. "Why wouldn't I be? Others have faith in me despite all your efforts."

"You think you're invincible."

He casually raised his shoulders. "I possess immunity and a loyal following. I will undoubtedly escape from this place. Rest assured, your efforts to impede me next time will be futile."

Irina nodded. "Why did you choose to aid us then? What made you decide to go along with our request?"

"I was terrified of death. It's natural for anyone to do whatever it takes to avoid it when they feel that fear."

"No. Only cowards act as you did. Nev never changed character when faced with death," Irina said.

Paul Randall clicked his tongue. "He is a fool. Rest assured, Irina. You will have a similar decision to make one day. And soon."

"What do you mean?"

"I have supporters with plans, and you have a weak leader. She was weak before the attack, but now . . . well, she's only weaker."

Irina's stomach twisted. "So, you're not fearful, even with me here."

He laughed. "You wouldn't defy your leader, as much as you despise me."

"And that's the reason I've come," she said, reaching into her pocket and producing the strange contraption. "Do you have any idea what this is?"

"A grenade?"

"It's a new invention. A mist. It releases little droplets when opened, choking whoever is in its vicinity within thirty seconds." She paused. "But you know that already. You added them to your first implants. Then you started developing these contraptions before you were imprisoned."

He pushed himself upright, trying to get his feet under him. "You wouldn't."

Irina paused before speaking. "You would do it," she said. "Earlier, a thought came to me. I realized that I can't spend my life worrying about you. I'd rather live without the constant worry that you might engage in some theocratic nonsense again than live in fear. I'll take that risk if I don't have to worry about my friends and family."

"What about ethics, Irina? Isn't that what you Shield people pride yourselves on?"

"Maybe that's true, but I believe in staying true to my individual beliefs rather than conforming to group thinking. I prefer to call it the code of hope."

Paul's face visibly paled. "We can surely find a way to agree . . ." he stammered.

Irina had heard enough.

She pulled the release, tossed it into the room, and slammed the door, closing her eyes to block out the horrific sound of Paul screaming and wailing. Once he went utterly quiet, she didn't linger a second longer. She swiftly made her way to the elevator, steadying her nerves as her hands quivered uncontrollably, then passed by the guards on the ground floor as if everything were normal.

After putting significant distance between herself and headquarters, the relentless heat bearing down on her, she sought refuge in a narrow alley that was heavily shadowed. She was overcome with intense nausea that forced her to double over and vomit. Her nerves were wounded, and she struggled to comprehend the magnitude of what she had just done. She had taken lives before while participating in missions with The Shield, but that was somehow different. It was a means of survival and in the moment, but this . . . She had attacked another while they were a sitting duck. Was that also survival? Her mind raced. She was sure that Paul posed a danger now and into the future, and if she hadn't acted, his devoted followers would relentlessly pursue his release or seek retribution. The cycle would never end.

Deep down, she knew what she had done was necessary and crucial. She had to move. Act normal. The store. Candy. Movie night with the group.

Summoning all her courage, she steeled herself before emerging onto the sidewalk. She strolled up a block to the newly renovated stores, their facades crafted from a muted grayish brick. Irina lowered her gaze, determined to avoid eye contact with passersby as her thoughts whirled.

The sight of sparsely stocked shelves caught her eye as she entered, a common occurrence since Paul Randall had taken over. However, now at least there were a few new shipments on display. Sour candies in various vibrant colors, a small bag of decadent chocolates, some crispy chips. She grabbed two bags of each item and headed to the checkout. The middle-aged cashier peered over her glasses as she approached. The store felt warm, with off-white tiles and a faint smell of packing boxes.

A woman burst through the door, breathless and wide-eyed. "Paul Randall is no more!"

The cashier's eyebrows shot up as she exclaimed, "What?!"

"Dead!"

"How?"

"Poison or something of the sort. That's what they're saying."

Irina focused on regulating her breath; her ears perked, picking up every sound. "Have they identified the perpetrator?"

The woman's response was calm as she shrugged. "No, they don't appear to be putting in much effort to find them."

The cashier's laughter rang through the air, filled with relief and joy. "I finally feel safe."

The woman smiled warmly, tucking her blonde locks behind her ear. "Rebecca might not be happy about it, but . . ."

"Rebecca will be pissed," Irina blurted out.

The two women looked at her. "You're Irina," the cashier said.

Irina nodded.

"I expected you to be the one who'd eliminate him after all the stories of your doings during his rule."

Irina chuckled. "Well, someone managed to do it before I could. I was on snack duty."

It was surprisingly simple to fabricate the lie.

"That you were," the cashier said, giving her a small knowing wink.

ABOUT THE AUTHOR

Jordyn Fleming is a passionate writer and storyteller with an MA in English and Creative Writing. She is also a member of the International English Honor Society, Sigma Tau Delta. From an early age, Jordyn was captivated by the world of books, spending countless hours lost in stories that sparked her imagination. She enjoys creating imaginative realms, diving into the rich worlds of speculative and fantasy fiction where the impossible becomes possible, and the ordinary transforms into the extraordinary. When she isn't writing, Jordyn loves spending time with her beloved French bulldogs, exploring new movies, and attending live concerts. Her debut fantasy novel, *Blade of Queens*, is coming soon. Connect with Jordyn on Instagram @jordynflemingwriter.